SAVAGE LOVE

SCOURGE SURVIVOR SERIES – BOOK SIX

JL MADORE

Savage Love / JL Madore -- 1st ed.

ISBN 978-1-990853-09-8

To the folks at 20Books for all their shared support, experiences, and wisdom. Michael and Craig inspire us to get words on the page every day.

A QUOTE I FOUND INTERESTING

Wolves no longer live in Oklahoma, according to the Oklahoma Archeological Survey. The state's bounty hunting decimated bison population and reduced deer population until the complete elimination of wolves in the 1930s.
Unsubstantiated rumors of wolf sightings still occur periodically, according to the Oklahoma State Game Wardens Association Magazine.

CHAPTER ONE

*M*y head cranked around on my neck, the pain of gauntlet to jaw bringing the bite of tears to my eyes. Blood burst from my lip in a macabre spray, my adrenaline ratcheting up from mildly interested to growing amusement. Ten against two was hardly fair, but our opponents' drunken fog seemed to negate Kobi's warning that this wouldn't end well for them.

Ducking the strike of the wooden leg of a barstool, I spun and punched. My knuckles buried hard into flab, my opponent's makeshift club clattering to the sticky dance floor along with the flannel-clad tough-guy who thought he had things all figured out.

Kobi snorted behind me, the demon's odd sense of humor triggered by a clumsy display of his attackers colliding off one another like something from a Three Stooges skit.

"Stop the clowning around, you two," Suzi snapped from behind the bar. "Take out the trash or I will."

The namesake and owner of Psycho Suzi's cocked the sawed-off in her hand and raised a silver brow. Suzi topped the list as the toughest female I'd had the pleasure of working with and considering the depth of field that category held—Blaze, Lexi, and his sister, Zophia—that said a lot about the woman.

If she were forty years younger, I'd be in love.

Shit. I grabbed Kobi and pulled my brother-in-arms out of the path of a sucker punch rushing in from three o'clock.

He scowled. "I saw that coming, Sav."

Yeah, right. I rolled my eyes and raised my hands. *Next time, I'll let them steamroll you onto the floor.*

Kobi eyed the worn, drink-drenched parquet and snorted. "Yeah, that's just gross."

Back at it, grunts and groans escaped the mob of men falling at the soles of their shitkickers like late-night worshippers. By the worried grimaces from the no-longer-cheering section, these studs promised to impress the ladies by taking out the leather-clad hardasses.

Ha. Sucked to be them.

Kobi's phone went off, and the generic ringtone was weird. Having a song dedicated to every person in his contact list got him razzed on the regular, or beaten if the caller didn't appreciate the associated dedication.

My ring was "Bad to the Bone." I approved.

Heat sliced my side. *Shit.* I spun, and the barroom brawl returned to the forefront of my attention. Dumb-fuck bastard. I grabbed the hilt of the switchblade lodged above my left hip and pulled it free.

Kobi's eyes flipped to scarlet, his mask to hide his demon side discarded. He finished off his final opponent with a palm thrust and a broken nose. The crunch of cartilage had the crowd groaning and the girls letting off little whimpers of distress. "Not cool, asswipe," Kobi snapped. "Why go to weapons. We were having a nice little Donny-brook, and you went and ruined it."

I barely heard my buddy's words. Fury fired in my gut, the acid burn of bile in my throat overshadowing all reason. After more than a decade of fighting the most powerful and vile enemy imaginable, did this asshat think *he'd* be the one to take me down?

Not bloody likely.

Fed up with the whole encounter, I grabbed two guys by the ankles, Flashed outside, and dumped them on the porch. When I stormed back inside, I grabbed two more.

Rinse and repeat.

Me dematerializing clued a few idiots into the fact that I wasn't an average Joe biker hanging at the bar. Few citizens of the Realm of the Fair possessed that ability: gods, Weres, and Talon warriors.

Two out of fucking three assholes.

The heel of my size sixteens stomped the sac of Stabby-Mc-stabber man, and the tough guy with the mullet curled up like a boiled shrimp. Another trip outside and I slammed the door to shut them out in the cold.

Harsh night, all the way around.

The violence didn't faze the patrons who cleared the dance floor to watch the fight. In this realm, and especially in the communities of Haven Mountain, everyone had pretty much seen or suffered every nightmare imaginable. The late-night socialites flooded back onto the dance floor and picked up their two-step shuffle, the altercation forgotten.

Back at our booth, I hiked up my wet tee to assess the damage. Fucking hell. Couldn't a guy go out for a few dozen drinks with a pain in the ass buddy without ending up on the pointy end of some wannabe tough guy's poker?

Kobi ass-planted across the table and eyed the damage. "Stop whining. It's a flesh wound, you pussy."

I flipped him a skull-ringed bird. Mutes didn't complain much, and I wouldn't if I could. Where was the style in it?

"Let's not tell Zo about this, 'kay? She's pissed that I danced around what I was doing when I left tonight. You getting shanked at Suzi's wouldn't win me any points."

I lifted my eyebrow. *I'm surprised you've got points left to lose.*

Kobi checked the scuffed flesh on his knuckles and laughed. "I'm new to the whole marriage thing, but honestly, I think I'm rocking it. Not to get into TMI but your sister is a highly satisfied woman these days. Between Aust and I—"

I drew my heat; twin Glocks pointed across the table. My BFF, and recent brother-in-law stopped flapping his jaw and laughed. "Techy.

My *point* is that we're solid." He smiled at his own words. "Yeah, baby, so fucking solid—"

I flicked the safeties off and set the guns at the ready. *Not another word, demon. I swear the next indecent image of my sister popping into my head earns you lead.*

Kobi busted up, his platinum piercings catching the tavern light as he threw his head back. "If you shoot me, they'll rush to my aid to heal me. Gotta say, with what the three of us get into, it would be *soooo* worth the hit."

I fucking hate you. I abandoned the idea of shooting him, refusing to be the cause of some mass orgy threeway with my sister and her two husbands.

From what I heard, Aust, Kobi, and my sister, are a match made in the heavens. Her marrying two men kinda struck me stupid. It wasn't like I was a prude or anything, I just didn't get it.

I was happy for all three of them—well, it weirded me out that my sister was sexing it up with Kobi—but almost completely, solidly happy for them. Three in a marriage just felt like a recipe for a complicated life. After all I plowed through over for almost two decades, complicated wasn't what I craved.

"Nice face on you," Kobi said, leaning back against the wall. "Seriously though, you should come home with me and crash. Surely, the way we warriors live, your soul-searching can't be that involved. With the cray-cray of the holidays over, the coast is clear."

Oh, the holidays. I considered returning home for the festivities but knew I'd stall out under the mistletoe in the entrance of Jade's mansion. She decked out the entire place in white lights and greenery, and I couldn't face it. A guy needed to build up defenses, to keep everyone's Yule spirit from sweeping him out to sea in a monstrous riptide of cheer.

Suzi joined us with a tray of drinks, a damp cloth, and a well-battered first aid kit we raided on the regular. It really should have our names on it, with little notches for each time we needed to use it. "You better not mention this to that new wife of yours, Kobi. She might put you on a leash."

Kobi laughed and waggled an ebony, platinum-pierced brow. "We were discussing that very issue, Suzi. Although, masochist that I am, I love bondage, and Zo's a wildcat when she's mad. The other night, she stripped me down and—"

My gun went off, and Kobi's shoulder hit the back wall of the booth from the impact.

The demon's head cranked around like something from *The Exorcist*. His eyes glowed scarlet, the flames of Hell bringing his demon side to the surface. "Fuck you, Savage. That hurt."

I set my smoking Glock on the table and felt no regret. I told him not to get into sexual specifics with me sitting there. I barely knew my sister.

Who wanted images like that stuck in their head?

Kobi shucked off the sleeve of his jacket, checked that the slug had passed straight through, and grabbed a roll of gauze. "That was dirty pool. I wasn't even talking to you, asshole. I was speaking to Suzi."

Still my sister. Still don't want to hear it.

"All right, boys, I'll leave you two to duke this one out." Suzi nodded to a server at the bar and left us to our Good Housekeeping patchwork session.

I opted for liquid sedation before addressing the ooze warming my hip. I refilled my tumbler and then slid Kobi the bottle. I was a gentleman like that.

"You need to get laid," Kobi groused, shoving the medical supply kit my way. "This self-induced sexual dry spell you're rocking has made you into a fucking bear. What happened to the guy who'd bang two or three chicks a night? That guy could party. Having troubles down yonder, buddy?"

This time, I aimed at his crotch. *Stop thinking about my cock. Right now, or I'll shoot you again. Have you considered that I might know how to be discreet? It's a concept lost on you, I know, but not everyone hangs their junk out for everyone to see.*

"I pity those who don't. And no, you aren't discreet. I'm an Incubus, dumbass. I sense sexual frustration. I'd smell if a female has been getting you off. You're too long on the road, big fella. Time to head on in and wet your whistle. And when I say whistle, I mean your cock."

I leaned back and shook my head. *I wish I could quit you. I really do.*

"Lies." Kobi snorted. "You luuuurve me."

"Yeah, we thought we'd find you two here." I followed the melodious chime of a choir's song and met the gaze of my half-sister, Zophia. A pure-blood Fae goddess, she was a stunner despite the disguise of mundane clothes and makeup she wore when leaving the sanctuary grounds of Haven.

I nodded to Aust at her side and figured it was my duty as Kobi's fellow soldier to fall on the sword. *Hey, sis,* I said straight into her mind. The god channel we shared negated the need for hand signals, which I didn't mind now that I was used to it. *Not his fault. I asked him not to say anything.*

"Uh-huh. And what have you boys been up to tonight?"

With the adrenaline of the fight dissipated, the brilliant red of Kobi's demon side had drained away. It left only the Goth GQ chic of a man in leather and guyliner. He looked up at his mates, and the rush of adoration that colored his face was nothing I ever expected from the demon. "Nothing much. A few drinks, a bar brawl, oh, and Sav shot me."

Totally thrown under the bus. *I warned you twice. It wasn't like you didn't know it was coming. Besides, it's just a chicken wing. Now, who's whining, pussy?"*

The demon's phone rang again. This time, the Celtic tune, "Men Behind the Wires," came on and Kobi pulled it out to answer. "Hey, Julian, what's doing?"

While Kobi chatted with ground control, I wiped things clean, avoided eye-contact with my sister, and finished with the butterfly tape. This wasn't the first hole I'd plugged in my side and wouldn't be the last. I dropped my shirt over the damage and reclaimed my glass, giving the concerned on-lookers a thumbs up.

Zophia signaled for Kobi to shove over and Aust grabbed a chair, flipped it around, and straddled it at the end of the booth. After topping up Kobi's glass, my sister took a long swig and pointed at my side. "If you reclaimed your abilities, patching yourself up would be a moot point."

Yeah, Castian gave me back what my brother stole, but I wasn't sure I wanted to open that door. Activating that side of my gene pool weirded me out. *For fifteen years, I've been fully mortal, fighting the fight, bleeding, aging—all the good stuff. I think I've done all right.*

"Maybe you fought so long and focused so hard on stopping Abaddon, now that the battle is won, you don't know what to do with yourself."

I bit back the growl and looked around for our server. As a Fate, Zophia's insights rang far too accurate for my liking. I preferred to be the aloof, broody stranger in the corner. Not front and center being psychoanalyzed.

The skillset of a heartless assassin doesn't translate into everyday life. I'll re-slit my throat before accepting a desk job or anything at the academy.

In truth, teaching physical combat didn't totally suck. After wiping the blood off my fingers, I reclaimed my tumbler and went back to numbing my brain. Enough social outing for one night. I needed to commit to the task at hand.

Kobi would be happy enough to call things early and head home with Zo and Aust. I glanced over to my wingman to see how he was doing on the phone.

"Tonight? It's fucking Oklahoma cattle country, Julian. What could happen between now and the dawn of the morning?"

Jack Daniels caught in my throat and I spat spray and sputtered on the burn. Trouble brewing in Oklahoma cattle country brought rolling nausea to my gut and a tightening to my cock. Which was crazy. Oklahoma was a big state and odds were that the trouble had nothing to do with—

"Why isn't Cowboy handling it?"

I cursed inwardly, my grip tightening on my glass. Okay, but Cowboy's old wolfpack had caused trouble before. It still didn't mean that it had anything to do with Hann—

"Hannah Burke? Who the fuck is that?"

The hair on my arms stood on end.

"Yeah, I got it." Kobi rolled his eyes as if he was bored while my heart ricocheted like a rogue pinball in my chest. "I *got* it. Fuck off. I said I'll take care of it."

I poured myself another round and tried to still the tremor in my hands before the ever-watchful gaze of Zophia noticed I was wigging out. I tipped back the glass and chugged. The empty came down on the pitted surface of the table with a crack, and I lifted my hands. *So, what's doing in Oklahoma?*

"Some woman called an old cell number of Cowboy's that Julian rerouted. She left the wolf a message that there was an emergency with his parents and he needed to get home."

Cowboy's parents? *Why should he give two shits about those assholes?*

Kobi tossed cash on the table and shrugged. "Don't shoot the messenger, Sav. I've already got one hole I didn't ask for tonight, fuck-you-very-much."

Aust eyed the seepage staining Kobi's gauze wrap and frowned. "You should come home to heal, not venture off to aid people who beat their own son and left him for dead."

"Trust me, Highborne," Kobi said, his smile more intimate than should be allowed in public. "I'd much rather come home and heal, but I'm the lucky bastard who gets to follow up. Bruin's at a Were Summit in Africa and Cowboy's there as his Beta. They're out of communication for the next couple of days. I drew the short straw."

I shook my head and gathered my guns. After holstering them at the small of my back, I changed the program. I loved the incubus demon but wouldn't let him anywhere near Hannah—especially when he had a wound to heal. *You three go home. I've got it.*

Kobi lit up. "Seriously?"

I met the demon's fist for a bump. *It's the least I can do. I shot you, remember?*

"I vaguely recollect the bullet searing through my flesh."

Shifting to get out of the booth, I waited until Aust stood to clear my path. Gods, even those quick seconds seemed to tick into hours. I needed to lock my shit down.

"Safe home, Savage," Aust said, dropping his chin.

I squeezed the guy's shoulder and gave my sister a nod. *Laters all.*

"Before you go." Zophia rose and stepped in front of me. Even with her opal skin covered and wearing a hoodie and jeans, there was no way anyone with half a brain wouldn't know she was extraordinary. Her powers brought the very air around us to life.

She straightened and wasn't far off meeting me eye to eye. "Promise you'll come home when you're finished this assignment. I'm not the only one who misses you. Jade and Lexi ask about you all the time, and with you not here for training, the men are getting a little soft around the middle."

"Rude." Kobi snorted. "Accurate, but still rude."

The moment she brushed my mind privately, I felt her concern. *With no Scourge to battle and an unknown future, we're all a bit lost. You won't find your answers in a world of strangers. You'll find them here, with your family.*

I winced as I shrugged on my jacket, wondering if the hole in my hip would be an issue. A curvy blonde noticed me readying to leave and headed over. I waved off the interested party. My sights were set on the brunette who stole my cold, dark heart years ago.

Man, this evening had taken a one-eighty.

Glancing at the repacked antiseptics and gauze, I wondered if I should stash a few supplies in my pockets to go. Hannah was gonna tear me to shreds for darkening her door after how I left things. How could you want something so bad you tasted it, and also dread it with everything you had?

Was that normal?

"I'll walk you out and fill you in," Kobi said, following as I crossed the dance floor. "So, this Hannah woman. Julian said she runs a ranch on the opposite side of the creek from Cowboy's pack lands. Her dog caught a scent, and when she chased him down to Cowboy's old family farmhouse, she found a pair of male wolves with their throats torn out."

I focused on the neon sign in the door, hoping the brisk January weather would cure my sudden case of the tipsy-topsies. There was more. With this kind of shit, there was always more. And who wanted to bet that I wouldn't like it?

"But since *three* wolves should've been there, the woman was going out to search for the female—Cowboy's mother."

Fuck. Of course she was. Because when a defenseless human came across the slaughtered Alpha and begotten of a volatile pack of Werewolves, her first instinct screams for her to dive into a situation she knows nothing about and put herself in harm's way.

"You know how Weres are, Sav. If it's a changing of the guards, it's over. If there's more to it, and this woman gets between a bunch of bloodthirsty wolves and what they want, she'll end up shredded."

I missed the step and dropped off the wooden porch of the dive bar. The collision with the ground knocked the wind from my lungs. I fought not to lose my shit and met Kobi's concern with my own. *I get it. I'll keep her safe.*

"Hey, do the wolf deaths make Cowboy the new Alpha?"

I checked my watch. Almost three-thirty in the morning. Why the hell is Hannah out and about in the middle of the night anyway? *Would have—I suppose—if he wasn't dead.*

"They don't know he survived?"

I sighed at the twenty questions routine. *When everyone you love celebrates your elimination, it doesn't make for any warm fuzzies. Cowboy left them all in his dust.*

I learned that lesson but did the opposite. When my twin tortured me and left me for dead, I spent every moment of the next fifteen years tracking the bastard down to even the score.

Family you choose for the win. I held out my fist for the bump. *I'll check it out.*

"You sure? I bitched, but I can go. Or I can go with you."

I fought the urge to growl. *I'll have to clear my schedule, but I can squeeze in some family drama for our boy. I'll check in when I know something.*

"'Kay, I'll text you the addy."

After a quick nod, I threw my molecules into the night. I didn't need directions. I could find that ranch like a homing pigeon, my time there etched into my very DNA.

~

Hannah reined Whisky Jack to a stop and shielded her eyes from the blistering wind. Scanning past the herd huddled along the fence line, she searched for anything out of the ordinary to explain the knots in her gut. Her family land was her stomping grounds, her sanctuary. She never felt uneasy out here. Tonight—she did. With a winter storm blowing in, and a full moon shifting behind clouds overhead, shadows slinked across the pasture. Maybe it was the shock of finding Jed and Jessop dead, but she couldn't escape the ominous sense of foreboding.

She glanced back to the wolf lying motionless, wrapped and bound in Whisky Jack's blanket. The makeshift drag she'd fashioned behind her horse was crude but would do the trick long enough to get them back to the house. If Myra wasn't dead, she was darn close to it. From rescuing Waylon years ago, she'd learned that a Werewolf shifted back to their animal form when asleep, unconscious, or dead.

Myra wasn't napping, so whatever she suffered from, it wasn't good. Sadly, she had no idea how long her neighbor had lain on the icy creek bed by the time she found her.

Hannah drew a deep breath, and the cold ached in her lungs. Frigid Oklahoma winter chilled her nostrils, and she wished she could filter scents that came to her like the Weres.

What would she smell? Her horse, the herd, the dried wheatgrass of the main pasture, the creek beyond, and the evergreen forest beyond that? Would Myra's scent bring Jed and Jessop's killers straight to her door?

She prayed that the wind of the coming storm would buy her time. But the time for what? She couldn't take Myra to the doctor or the vet. The only thing she could think of doing was to get her inside and keep her safe and warm.

Chief barked beside Whisky's flank, and she startled. Her border collie growled, his head dipped low to the frozen ground, his hackles raised straight up. Following the dog's line of sight, she focused on the darkness west along the foothills. *Something wicked this way comes.*

Hannah gripped the reins tighter and got their party moving again. She didn't dare go too fast, not with Myra getting pulled along the ground behind. She shot a glance back to the shifting shadows.

Yep. Still coming.

"It's likely just a deer foraging before the storm, Chief. Nothing to worry about." Except it was half-past three in the morning, and with a winter storm brewing, the deer were hunkered down. Man, she couldn't even lie to herself.

Besides, whatever was stalking her didn't move with the tentative steps of a deer. Wishful thinking wouldn't change reality. It was a man —a big man.

Woodsboro Creek was home to more than its share of big men. Coming from the direction of Jessop's land, where she'd found the Alpha and his son, there was no doubt in her mind. A Were had tracked them down.

Hannah brought Whisky around and reached back for the stock of her rifle. When the gun rested across her lap, she took off her gloves, drew her sidearm, and checked her Colt.

Chief barked a second time, and she sympathized. "I know, boy, and you're right. But like Daddy always said, 'If you're goin' out,—best to go out fightin'.'"

Every warning bell she possessed clamored as she pocketed her handgun, raised the rifle, and sighted the lone man prowling toward her. In the pit of her stomach, she dreaded killing someone she knew. If this was pack politics, the killer or killers were people she'd known her entire life—maybe people she considered friends.

Sadly, that wouldn't work in her favor. These Weres believed in their pack above all else.

Humans were second-rate citizens.

Her only saving grace was that they didn't know that she knew about them. She was simply a good Samaritan lending a helping hand to an injured animal on her land. Her heart hammered as the figure drew nearer and she made out his features—Carter Hurley.

"Howdy, stranger," she said, her finger poised on the trigger of the rifle. She took in his easy stance, wishing it was lighter out, so she could gauge his animal's intent by the color of his eyes. "Mind if I ask what you're doin' on my land so late at night, Carter? You scared me half to death."

She didn't know the man well but knew enough. He'd come to town about eight months ago from somewhere out east. As a lone wolf, Jessop had taken him into the pack, and the rest of the town had accepted him after that. He'd gotten into a few scuffles at the local bar on Saturday nights, but other than being a hot-head drinker, he seemed all right.

Whisky Jack adjusted his footing and nickered, tossing his head so his mane batted against the suede sleeves of her jacket. The movement rocked her in her saddle, but she didn't let that affect her aim.

Carter remained locked in her sights, his relaxed body and sly smile implying he was out for a leisurely stroll in the country. It didn't fool her for a second.

The vicious growl behind her came out of nowhere.

Before she could turn, something hard and heavy struck her back and toppled her from her horse. She hit the ground hard, shrieking as her wrist bent at an awkward angle.

As pain overtook her, everything happened at once. Whisky bolted past her, and she rolled to keep from being trampled. Carter yelled and lunged to catch the horse's bridle. Chief turned, snapping and snarling at a massive silver wolf. And her good hand fell against the smooth walnut stock of her rifle. Rolling onto her stomach, she reached to grab it.

Carter kicked it out of her reach and *tsked* her for trying. "Now, Miss Hannah. Settle yourself."

She called Chief back. Her old pup was brave but had no chance against a Werewolf. After a few more heated calls, he obeyed and closed ranks, bending low with his teeth bared.

The wolf prowled past her and rounded Whisky Jack toward the drag. Her pulse rushed in her ears. Weres were massive beasts. Terrifying. Breathtaking. They pretty much made her pee her pants. She'd only been this close to one once and that was more than a decade ago.

The wolf nuzzled Myra's bundle, growling long and low.

Carter secured her rifle and shook his head. "Now, what have you done to poor old Myra?"

"Myra?" she said, laying as much confusion into her voice as she thought she could pull off. "What are you talking about? I found that wolf unconscious in the creek. I was taking it to the pen in the drive shed to get her warm and dry."

Carter pulled the folds of the blanket back to examine its contents. "She didn't say anything to you?"

Hannah squinted at him, the pain in her arm making it hard to keep a clear head. "The wolf? What exactly do you think she would say?"

The darkness of night kept Carter's face in the shadows. "Come on, Hannah. The pack has suspected for years that you know what we are. Jessop may have protected you, but that's over now."

Hannah swallowed. She'd always been on friendly terms with Jessop but didn't know he'd protected her. All the more reason to try to save his wife. "I couldn't leave her in the creek to die."

"That's exactly what you shoulda done. Now you've gone and meddled in pack business. What were you even doing out this time of night? You woulda been all right if you were warm in your bed."

Hannah was dead. Even without a broken wrist, she couldn't defeat two Werewolves. They were preternatural creatures with enhanced strength and heightened senses. The only thing she could do was to try to convince them she'd only been innocently trying to help Myra.

Not that it would work.

"The storm came up outta nowhere," Hannah said, her breath escaping in white puffs of cloud. "I needed to bring the cattle in before it hit. Chief caught wind of Myra's scent and took off. I followed and was taking her home to warm up."

"And that's it? That's the whole story?"

She blinked and nodded. Weres could smell lies, but with the wind swirling and carrying on in the opposite direction, she'd risk it. "I swear."

"Then why pull a gun on me?"

"A man came up on me in the dark when I'm alone. Why wouldn't I pull a gun on you?"

Carter frowned. "Your scent is rife at Jessop's farmhouse so you can cut the innocent act. You know more than you're saying and we both know it. How dumb do I look?"

Lying had never been her strong suit. Might as well go with truth. "Dumb enough that I thought I might have a shot."

Carter stomped forward, pinning her broken wrist under his boot. She gasped, the agony excruciating. Her vision blacked out and then burst into white splotches behind her eyes. He stepped harder and the bones ground together under his heel.

Her scream echoed across the flat plane of the main pasture and darkness narrowed her field of vision. Chief whined, and she pressed her face into his cold, snow-crunchy coat. "S'okay, boy."

"You shoulda minded your own, human."

Hannah blinked past her tears, and her future flashed briefly. He had no intention of her living. She would die, right there in the field. Riley would be alone and defenseless. Alone in a vast, empty farm-house on the edge of town . . . what would he do to her. Would he go for her next or end it here?

"Don't do this." She inched her fingers toward the Colt bruising her hip. "You *know* me. You don't want to do this. I've got my kid sister to raise . . . this farm to run."

Carter kicked her shoulder and rolled her. The force of the momentum tore the gun from her feeble grip, and it clattered at his feet. A second later, Carter aimed it straight at her head. "You shoulda thought about that before you messed in pack business."

Hannah closed her eyes.

The shot cracked in the air, and everything went black.

CHAPTER TWO

I took out the Were with the gun first. The shot to his shoulder spun him away from Hannah and with the crack of his neck, the male fell to the ground and morphed into his base form. Adrenaline exploded in my veins. Hannah lay helpless on the cold ground, and I had no idea how badly she was hurt. I readied for the wolf's attack—welcomed it. The sooner this was over, the sooner I could assess her injuries and help her.

The silver timber wolf advancing, stood smaller and less muscled than Cowboy. I had no doubt I could hold my own one-on-one. I'd tussled with Bruin and Cowboy enough over the past decade to know what to expect. Hell, Bruin transformed into an oversized Kodiac.

After facing that, nothing much worried me.

This opponent, however, had no idea what he faced. The wolf would overestimate his skills, and that would be his undoing. As the beast charged, I drew the dagger sheathed to my thigh and Flashed to the side. Grappling the thick ruff of his coat, I severed its throat.

Quick and dirty.

The eerie yelp carried on the wind long after I pivoted and lodged the blade deep into the beast's chest. Heaving for breath, I went down with the weight of my kill and rested on one knee. Grabbing a handful of snow, I brushed my gloves clean and shifted to where Hannah lay waaaay too still on the ground. Two fingers against Hannah's neck gave me no pulse.

Fear plunged into my heart as sharp as my dagger into the wolf. *How? No!* Panic sucker punched me so hard I felt it push its way into my lungs, expanding, taking the place of oxygen until I fought for short, quick hits of air. No matter how I gasped and panted, I couldn't breathe.

I wanted to fight. I wanted to kill these men again.

A muffled groan brought me back to sense and my entire body sagged with relief. Stupid dumbass. I pulled my gloves off and tried for the pulse with my brain in the game this time.

Strong and steady. Thank the gods.

I flopped onto my ass and waited until the shakes cleared. Why was it I could never think straight around this woman? She was my emotional Kryptonite but at the same time, my addiction. I tried not to think about how badly I'd tanked the relationship and got back to the situation at hand.

What were we dealing with? Judging by the flaxen and caramel pelt, the wolf bundled behind the horse might very well be Cowboy's mother. I crawled over to where the wolf lay, and placed a hand against her chest to gauge her breathing. Weak and thready.

Hard to say if that was a win or a loss.

Returning to Hannah's still form, I surveyed the land and assessed my options. It would be light soon, so I needed to hurry. I could save Hannah and erase the mother from the equation. I could leave the mother with the other bodies and let the Weres have their fun. Or, I could save them both and let the Fates decide.

I chuffed. Yeah, the Fates would pick whatever result screwed the most people—preferably me. My self-absorbed, self-serving, self-righteous half-sisters were vengeful bitches, and Zophia and I were currently high on their shit-list.

The gutted wolf's blood steamed from the ground as I mulled things over. Choices, choices. Hannah's dog rubbed against my hip, and I scrubbed the pup's ears. *Hey, Chief. What do you think we should do?*

The dog whined and nuzzled Hannah with his snout.

Yeah, me too. Gathering Hannah off the thin layer of snow, I Flashed across the pasture and into the ranch house. After setting her on the couch, I unzipped her coat to examine her injuries. The line of her clothes hugging her curves stole my breath and scrambled my thoughts.

Right. Injuries. A couple of scrapes and a bruise coming up on her cheek. Her wrist took the brunt of the damage and was swelling fast. Running my hands down her body to check for injuries flipped my train to another track entirely. This was why surgeons weren't allowed to operate on their loved ones, right? No objectivity.

My clinical assessment hadn't lasted long—which wasn't my fault. C'mon, look at her. Bundled for a ride in the country, Hannah was an attractive woman.

Once you undid things and got down to the cling of her knit sweater and the way her jeans hugged her curvy hips, yeah, she was a cock-hardening knockout.

Static spiked her chestnut hair as I tugged off her hat. With a gentle hand, I tamed it down. Still soft as silk. Just like that, all the feels and memories buried and barricaded for three years resurfaced.

Drawing a finger over the scuff on her cheek, I marveled that I'd been able to stay away from her this long. I closed my eyes, reliving the sound of her voice, the feel of her lush, generous curves, the scent and taste of her bronze skin. Yeah, time and distance hadn't dimmed anything from my memory.

Growling at myself, I got back to it. *I'll be back, baby. You're safe now.*

The drive shed door creaked as I opened it, the hinges not hanging level. I made a mental note to fix that and Flashed back to the pasture with the tools. Leaving shovels beside the dead wolves, I patted Chief and mounted the horse.

I rode to the barn, Cowboy's mother bumping and bouncing along behind the horse at a healthy clip. Sure, I could Flash her inside as I did with Hannah, but I wasn't feeling that charitable. A few bruises would do her good. After what Cowboy suffered, it was the least she deserved.

I steered Hannah's horse into an empty stall. There was fresh water in his bowl, and I dished a healthy scoop of feed into the trough. I'd come back and unsaddle him once I took care of the other honey-do items on the list.

After securing the stall latch, I closed the barn up.

I Flashed the wolf's mother inside the drive shed and threw a couple of old horse blankets into the large cage built into the corner. After setting up a heat lamp to keep her from freezing, I Flashed back to the house to check on Hannah.

Still out.

Stepping over to the stone hearth, I started a fire. Once the wood crackled, I got Chief settled next to her and headed back to the scene of carnage.

This was going to be a bitch.

I peeled off my leather jacket and tossed it to the snow, then drove the metal blade of the shovel an inch into the frozen earth.

January digging—fun.

Most people thought that being a warrior to the god of gods was an enviable position filled with perks. I swung the shovel and dumped the teaspoon of soil I managed to unearth. In actuality, the perks were few and far between. Being a Talon Enforcer meant sweat or blood most days. Somedays, like this one, it meant both.

I fingered the damp hole in my side where the timber wolf caught me with a lucky claw. The stab wound from earlier had opened and now bled through the bandaging.

Perfect.

And Kobi said I didn't know how to party.

Getting nowhere with the solid ground, I switched to Plan B. I Flashed the dead wolves behind the barn and started with the digging again. The slightly frozen crust on the manure pile was infinitely more obliging than frozen ground. It took no time at all to bury Hannah's dead attackers under a heaping pile of shit.

Karma was real.

~

Hannah came awake with a start and stilled. How did she get to the couch? Who took off her boots and coat? Her body ached as if she'd been trampled. She remembered the tackle off Whisky Jack. The fall. The attack. Where was Carter? Cradling her wrist, she swung her feet to the floor and had to stop while the world spun. Was he in the house? *Riley!*

On the coffee table beside her sat a bottle of painkillers, a glass of water, and her Colt. She went for the gun. It hurt like a bugger, but she managed to release the magazine and check. Still loaded.

An icy chill shot up the back of her neck. She rose unsteady, shuffling her socks against the old wood floor. Stumbling down the back hall, she closed the distance to the bedroom across the hall from hers.

Please, please, pleeeease, let her be all right.

Listing to the side, Hannah braced her good arm against the wall to stay upright. Riley's door was closed as she liked it. She turned the old glass knob and from the light of the descending moon, found her sister starfished and sprawled across her bed as always.

Except, it wasn't as always. Someone was in her house.

Closing the door, she lifted her gun, checked her bedroom, and then started a room-by-room search toward the front of the house. When she made it back to the open concept country kitchen/living room, she noticed the fireplace. Alit with the glow of orange flames, the living room welcomed her with an unsettling warmth considering the situation.

She studied the rounded mound of dark fur in front of the fireplace. Chief was sawing logs, his feet twitching as he chased dream livestock around the fields. How could he be sleeping? Her collie was much too protective to ignore an intruder. Did Carter leave her there and go?

Why? She was sure he would kill her.

Confused, Hannah sat back on the couch. She bumped her hand on the edge of the pine table, and the knock sent a surge of agony up

her arm. When the tears stopped stinging, she focused on the acetaminophen and water set out.

She swallowed four extra-strength tablets and clicked on the lamp.
There. Sitting in the shadows of the corner.

Him.

Their gazes locked and his expression hit, his midnight-blue eyes
as cold and volatile as the winter storm outside. Anguish squeezed her
lungs. Not a gentle squeeze, like the frail hug her dad had given her
before he passed. A sharp, suffocating squeeze. Like her horse bucking
and collapsing across her chest, crushing her against the unforgiving
ground.

He was the very last person she expected to find in her home—the
last person she wanted to confront as her entire body relived the
trauma of her attack.

"Get out."

Hannah leaned deeper into the back of the couch and crossed her
arms. A wave of panic hit, and it had nothing to do with the events of
the night. She reclaimed the blanket that had covered her and
breathed past the heaviness pressing on her chest. "I said, get out. I
don't want you here—*Steve.*"

He rose, like a dark lion stretching in the moonlight. She hoped he
might respect her wishes. Instead, he stopped at the island and poured
a cup of tea.

She didn't think it would be that easy—never was with him. But
tea? Really? Did he really think he could disappear for three years and
patch things up with Earl Gray?

As she scrambled around in her empty head, watching him go
through the milk and sugar motions, she couldn't decide which was
worse. The fact that he remembered how she liked it, or that he
looked so calm when everything inside her circled in a torrent of
emotion.

Dependent, weeping women who pined over the man who broke
their heart made her sick. She owed him nothing. He left her. No
explanation. No looking back.

No emotion showed on his harsh features, yet still, her adrenaline flared. With one brooding glance, her body lit with both anxiety and anticipation. It was always like that with him. One touch. One look. One step toward her and she was scrambling. As if on cue, he headed over with the tea.

It wasn't just herself she needed to protect this time around. She raised the gun. "Stay away from me."

Fury swept through her, strengthening her instincts of self-preservation. He had almost destroyed her. Not again. She was good on her own. They were good. The gun weighed heavily in her hand. What was she doing?

With the chaos of the night, maybe hysteria had set in.

She waved the barrel, and the man of her sexy nightmares stopped his approach halfway between her and the kitchen. Amusement crinkled the corners of his eyes, but he honored her wishes and waited for her to decide what to do.

What *would* she do? She wasn't about to shoot him for blowing her off—that was crazy. She felt a little crazy.

Okay, a *lot* crazy.

He studied her. Gawd, he had that see-right-through-you gaze she hated so much. "Stop looking at me like that. Eyes on the floor."

His acquiescence didn't fool her. An alpha male like him—driven and fueled by enough testosterone to choke a horse—only rolled over when he wanted to. He was letting her win. An apology, maybe?

She didn't need it. Didn't *want* it.

Still, her brain didn't muddle up so badly when he wasn't looking at her. At well over six foot and carrying the weight to fill out his muscled frame, he didn't fit a standard definition of handsome. No, that wasn't exactly true. He was brutally handsome—emphasis on brutal—as well as intensely masculine. Rugged. Chiseled. Strong.

The first time she'd seen him strutting down sunlit Main Street, with his dark-hair, dark-eyes, and covered in black leather and tattoos, he'd scared the bejeebers out of her. She'd darted into the hardware store to clear his path and hidden behind a rack of rope, tape, and fasteners.

When he answered her ad for a summer farmhand, he'd stood in the barn, and she'd had no place to run. She'd fallen for the man behind the aggression, and even though she accepted and adored him, he still didn't let her in.

Men. Always guarding their emotions like dark secrets tucked away in the back a of drawer.

He killed Carter. The realization popped into her head. She didn't know how she knew, but she did. Something sharper and more biting than alarm pierced Hannah's chest—indignation and fury stabbed her deep and hot. She'd been saved by *him*, by the man who all but killed her himself three years ago.

The lethal air that once scared her to death worked in her favor tonight. He'd come back from whatever hole he'd been hiding in and rescued her. She gave herself a quick inward shake. "Thanks for the save, but I asked you to leave."

He straightened, standing directly in front of her. Looming large, she felt the heat coming off him and the warmth of his breath. The smile curving his full lips looked no friendlier than he did. He set her tea down, lifted his hands, and—

She looked away. With her attention solidly focused on the things he'd set out for her on the coffee table, she threw him her frostiest look. "So, you break into my house and, while I lay helpless and vulnerable, you raid my medicine chest? I don't know why I have to say this, but you're no longer welcome in my personal space."

He gave her a sardonic smile, and it didn't matter that he didn't speak, she knew what he was thinking. It wasn't like he hadn't been in her bedroom or that bathroom before. How many nights had they enjoyed that big four-poster bed? How many mornings had they played in the shower together?

She couldn't think about that.

Her gaze dropped to his shirt hanging damp and pasted against his side. Was he hurt? Her foolish, pounding heart tangled in her chest. No. Stop. She didn't care. "Please, go. I'm too tired, and in too much pain to deal with you tonight."

He signed something, but she didn't look. She wanted to, and that made her more annoyed with herself. She had to be careful. She needed boundaries. Riley needed her to safeguard their future more than Hannah needed to cozy up to her most amazing mistake ever.

Images she'd locked away broke loose and reminded her how amazing. Wrestling in the hayloft, cooling off in the creek during long rides checking fences, picnic blankets under the willow. The man might not speak, but he had heightened ways of communicating.

She got up to pace. *Focus.*

To keep from dwelling on her weakness for him, she let loose the questions crashing around in her head. "What happened with Carter and that wolf? Where's Myra? How much trouble am I in? Why are you here? Now? Tonight?"

He curled his lip and got his hands moving. *Last one first. You're too reckless to keep yourself safe. Why the fuck would you challenge Weres alone at night? Are you crazy? You find two dead, and you go looking for the third?*

He didn't need a voice for her to hear the tone. She pointed a finger at his solid chest. "First off, the curse jar still has your name on it. Secondly, you don't get to judge me after you up and disappeared. I searched for you, you know? That's when I found out that everything you told me was a lie. Your childhood in New York, serving in the forces, even your name was a lie, *Steve.*"

At least he had the decency to look contrite. *That was for your protection as much as mine.*

Yeah, right. "You lied about everything and used me."

Bullshit. I kept my deets private but everything that happened between us was honest, and you know it.

She backed away, needing distance. Her headache gained ground from a steady beat to a throbbing drum. She wanted to lock herself in her room and lie down. "What world do you live in where your *name* is a personal detail you can't share with your lover?"

One hint, it's not the same world as the one you live in.

He'd given her the "our worlds are different" speech the day before he left. It was a cop-out then. It was a cop-out now. His rant from a moment ago played back in her mind. He'd said, *challenge Weres alone at night.* "How do you know about Werewolves and what I did? Are you spying on me?"

If I were, you wouldn't be nursing a broken hand.

"Yet you end up here at the very minute I need help?"

He scowled. *I'm just that fucking good.*

"Watch your tone. You don't want to take me on tonight." She huffed and swept the muzzle of her gun toward the door. "I'm not the girl I was three years ago. I don't accept hedging or half-truths from anyone. Either tell me what's going on or go and never come back."

A glint of fire flashed in his eyes, and she read the threat. Her heartbeat picked up in her chest, her trembling body responding to his broody gruffness more than it should. Getting thrown off Whisky rattled more than her teeth.

You're swaying, doc. You need to lay down and rest.

The endearment chipped away at her shield, and she fortified her resolve. "I need to get the cattle in before the storm hits full-on. That's why I was out there at three in the morning in the first place. I got them rounded into the inner-paddock, but they can't stay out."

You're in no shape to herd cattle.

"Tell that to my cattle. They'll die if it's as bad out there as they're predicting. Unlike you, I don't walk away and leave collateral damage behind."

He almost caught his reaction. The subtle recoil and tightening of his jaw were visible because she knew him as well as she did.

Fine. You rest, I'll bring them in.

"I don't need you to do my chores. I'm—"

Yeah, yeah, you're all that and more, but right now, you've got a broken wrist and were knocked off your horse, and almost killed. Get into bed. I've got this.

Part of her ached and wanted a hot bath. Another part of her—a part she didn't want to look at too closely—thought it served him right to be out in the cold. Not that he could make amends. "Do you even remember how to work the herd?"

I remember how to work everything on this ranch.

He pegged her with a gaze so heated, she looked away. "Well, you worked me over like a pro."

He shifted to get back into her line of sight. A genuine level of sorrow clouded his expression. *I'm sorry I left, doc. Seriously, I regret it every fucking day.*

Tired and a little woozy, she set down the gun, picked up her tea, and returned to the couch. The mug warmed her hand as she sipped against the rim. "After I found out everything you told me was a lie, you stopped mattering to me. You can stop regretting it—or let it eat at you. I don't care."

Let me explain.

"Why? I won't believe anything you say."

Hannah, on my honor as a soldier, I will never lie to you again. Not a half-truth. Not an omission for your own good. Nothing but the god's honest from now on. My work is done, my reason for leaving resolved. I'm here because I want to be, and I'm not going anywhere until you hear me out.

She didn't believe him. Sure, he sounded sincere, but the only person she could truly afford to believe in was herself—and Riley. The rest of the world paled in importance. "Okay, have your say. The first time I catch you in a lie, you're out the door and out in the cold."

He swallowed. *Understood.*

"Then tell me everything. Who you really are. Why you're here. Where you went. Why you came back. All of it."

He scowled. *It's late, and you've had a bad night. I'll answer three questions and then you're lying down. The rest will wait until tomorrow.*

She laughed. "Assuming you're still here."

I'll be here.

"That remains to be seen."

He pulled the club chair around to face her. *Go ahead—first question.*

Was he serious? Her mind whirled with a dozen things she needed to know, but she started with something simple. Something that meant nothing and yet meant everything to her. "What's your name? Your *real* name."

His scowl deepened.

She didn't care if he hated talking about himself, this would test whether or not he was capable of telling the truth. If it made him uncomfortable—all the better.

My birth name was Krastos, but I discarded it when my twin brother killed our mother, tortured me, and left me for dead. I adopted the name Savage ever after.

His brother what? The vulnerability in his eyes told her he wasn't making that up. Okay, she'd circle back to the horrors of childhood later. *Savage?* That's an adjective, not a name. Okay, two more questions. "How did you know to come here tonight?"

You called Cowboy's phone and left a message with the details of your sitch. He wasn't around, so I intercepted the follow-up order.

"Waylon?"

We know him as Cowboy. Where I'm from, almost everyone left one life behind to begin another.

For some reason, the idea that Waylon reinvented himself made her both happy and sad. She didn't blame him for starting over, but there was at least one person in Woodsboro Creek that cared for him and always would.

Maybe two, with the addition of Savage. If he was capable of caring for someone. He was a soldier first. If duty called, he'd be up and gone. She wouldn't delude herself into forgetting that. "All right, what are you here to do?"

Whatever is necessary to keep you safe. He didn't conceal the lethal threat in his words.

"*Us* safe. Me and Waylon's mother, right?"

You're out of questions, but I'll give you that one for nothing. Cowboy's mother doesn't figure into my concerns. If she survives, fine, but if wolves huff and puff and threaten to blow your house in, I'll point them to the drive shed and give her up in a heartbeat.

"Waylon won't approve of that."

If it comes down to you or her, he absolutely will.

Her tea had cooled enough that she could swallow it without burning her tongue. "What makes you think so?"

Ste—Savage leaned over the back of the chair and shrugged. *When we sign up for service, we each name anyone who matters from our previous life. It's a watchlist to ensure those left behind are safe. There is one person on Cowboy's list. You're the only person we're supposed to keep safe.*

She shook her head and set her mug on the coffee table. "I've known Waylon since we were kids. Somewhere deep inside, he cares if his mother lives or dies."

His family fucked him over because of a health condition he had no control over. They beat him and tried to kill him. Trust me, that's not a betrayal you forgive and forget.

The venom of his rant rang true. Savage wasn't talking about Waylon and the wolves anymore.

"So, what now?"

Now, you rest. You're out of questions. He pointed to the hall that led back to her bedroom. *I'll bring the cattle in. I've already taken care of your guests in the pasture, but when they fail to return, others will come. The weather should hold them off for a bit, but we need to figure out what's going on and take steps to ensure you're clear of the conflict. You need to be rested and at your best.*

Hannah sighed. She wasn't in any shape to be out herding cattle, and he was an adept farmhand despite him not looking the part. But how was a mute killing machine supposed to find out why a beloved pack alpha and his family were murdered?

Did he know what he was up against?

"No offense, but Waylon should take care of this."

Savage's lips turned up in a cruel smile. *You doubt that I'll keep you safe?* He dipped his chin, his gaze narrowing on her. He'd always been a big ball of angry, but someone or something had wound him up tight tonight.

He waited, glaring at her. She read the challenge in his gaze as if everything hinged on how she answered. "I have no doubt you're capable of protecting me. I simply think it's more Waylon's problem than yours."

Wrong. Like I said, everything that happened between us was honest. Like it or not, you're mine to protect. Mine to worry about. Mine to care for. Now, lay down and get a few hours rest. It'll be morning soon enough.

Mine? She wasn't chattel, and this wasn't the Dark Ages. His autocratic claim made her bristle in every direction, yet she couldn't disagree she needed to lay her head down and close her eyes. At least for a while.

~

I waited in the darkness of the front hall until Hannah was out cold, then moved to the couch to cover her up and tuck her in. When she first saw me in the shadows, I braced for her anger, but it didn't come. The fight I expected was strangled by sadness—disappointment in me —and regret burning in her daggered gaze. I fucked up, and it twisted my guts. I should have manned up and explained why I had to leave.

Except, if I laid it out and she still asked me not to go, I wouldn't have had the strength to leave her. I wanted to stay and let the problems of the world sort themselves out, but couldn't do it.

Staring down at her, I fingered the silky strands of long, brown hair and smiled as a curl wrapped around my finger. She might not realize she belonged to me, but her body did. Clinging to that one smoldering ember of hope, I tried to figure out how I could earn her trust back.

The look in her eyes when I claimed her highlighted how deep that hole I dug for myself went. I faced a steep uphill battle. Not that that scared me.

I kicked ass in battle.

Somewhere in the back of my mind, I believed if I explained why I left, she'd forgive me. Now, I wasn't so sure.

The glow of firelight dance across her scuffed cheek and I growled deep in my chest. If Hannah hadn't been in imminent danger, I would've liked to kill that fucker slow and with an enormous amount of pain.

Oh, the regrets of rash decisions.

Before heading out, I drank in one last look. How could a person be both incredibly delicate and resiliently tenacious at the same time? How sexy was it that she held me at gunpoint?

I smiled. I'd gladly take a bullet if it eased the pain of my betrayal.

After clicking off the lamp, I grabbed her chunky knit scarf and gathered my jacket off the back of one of the antique kitchen chairs.

With a smack to my thigh, Chief jumped up and joined me for the outing. Despite what I said, I needed help. Good thing Chief never turned down a chance to have some fun in the fields.

The bite of the wind slapped my face. I pulled on my gloves and tied Hannah's scarf around my ears and mouth. I'd never been one for the cold and this was brutal.

It worked in my favor that I hadn't unsaddled the horse. The brawny chestnut was ready to head back outside and get to work. This would suck, but the obstinate male in me reveled in the knowledge that I was out suffering in the storm and she was safe, warm, and resting.

Who said chivalry was dead?

CHAPTER THREE

*H*annah couldn't sleep in if she tried. Born and raised on this farm, her internal clock established itself decades ago. Chores to be done. Animals to be fed. Fences to be checked. Supplies at the Co-op to pick up. A rancher's workday stretched out from before dawn until after dusk. And then there was Riley. Raising a budding teen was a full-time job as well. She loved every minute of both, but she was tired.

Waking up tired on a four-thousand-acre ranch was a bad sign. Eyes closed, she gave herself a moment. The world outside raged, wild and feral. The wind screeched against the side of the sprawling bungalow. The double-hung windows rattled in their paint-encrusted frames. And the creaks and knocks of the roof and walls suggested the old house was wore out too.

Lying there, assessing her surroundings, she felt him.

Whether it signaled she remained that attuned to him or gotten used to waking up alone, his presence ignited a warm tingle beneath her skin. All kinds of hot and heavy ideas of how to spend a snow day came to mind. How long had it been since her body heated, aware of a man?

Oh, about three years.

She blinked against the gray of dawn, and yep, Ste—dammit —*Savage* overflowed Granny Jean's rocking chair in the corner of her bedroom. Snoring softly, her black knight slept, a gun resting on each of his thighs. She'd talk to him about that. With Riley around, she obsessed about gun storage and keeping things locked in the gun cabinet.

He, of course, didn't know about her yet.

How would they take to each other? He wasn't a nurturing guy. Who was she kidding? He was hard and scary most of the time . . . but there were moments when she'd seen his soft and gooey insides.

At least she thought she had.

She shifted against her mattress and frowned. She'd fallen asleep on the couch, and here she was, on her bed. Lifting the quilt, she let off a worried breath, pleased she still wore the clothes from last night. So, even though he claimed she was *his*, he didn't think he had carte blanche control over what went on with her.

Good. He wasn't welcome back like he never left. It would serve him right if she had a hunky fiancé heating her sheets at night. She didn't, but it would serve him right.

It wasn't that she wasn't open to falling in love and settling down— that would be great—but Woodsboro Creek was a small town. Without wanting to, she knew everything there was to know about every bachelor in town. Who they took to high school dances, if their team went all-state, who drank too much, who slept around too much—*everything*.

Nobody sparked her interest. No one measured up.

Savage's broody, soul-tormented air had sucked her in. Now it seemed to be the only thing that riled her up. When they were together, she wanted to help him work through his issues. She thought she'd shown him he could trust her.

And then he left.

Fool me once, shame on you. Fool me twice—nope, she wouldn't go through that again. Her life was complicated enough without taking on an emotionally distant fixer-upper.

If she let her heart get away from her, she'd be piecing it back together. Again. For Riley's sake, she'd keep this simple and fight their sexual pull. Her sister needed her to set an example and focus on saving the farm and feeding the herd through the winter.

She could do this.

She could stick to the business at hand—find out what happened with Myra and the wolves, and keep him at arm's reach. Yeah, right. Well, she could try. Hannah sat up and sucked in a breath as hot shards of pain shot up her arm.

Savage moved so fast she didn't register how he'd gone from sleeping in the chair to crouched in front of her, panning the room with his weapons.

"Sorry," she said, cradling her wrist. "I wanted to check on Myra and get chores started. I forgot about my wrist. Did you splint this?"

Savage holstered his guns at the small of his back and nodded, looking half-asleep. *Does it hurt bad?*

The mercurial shift from killer to concern made her head spin. One minute, he was ready to gun down anyone who came in the door, the next, he looked like he wanted to plump her pillows.

"I'm good—unless you can magically fix my wrist and make it stop hurting, then yeah, let's do that."

His strange expression made her wonder what he was thinking. With him, she always wondered what he was thinking. A shiver racked him. He tried to shake it off, but she saw he wasn't comfortable.

"You're soaking wet." She remembered his promise to bring in the cattle before the storm. It looked like he didn't get done before it hit. "Mercy, your hands are like ice."

She pressed a hand to his stubbled cheek, and he leaned into the contact. The unnatural warmth of his brow had her frowning and patting his shirt. "Why didn't you get out of these wet clothes?"

I didn't bring a change and didn't think you'd appreciate me rocking the Full Monty when you woke up.

"I won't appreciate you dying of pneumonia because of me either. I'll run you a hot bath. Get out of those clothes."

He flashed her a lascivious smile. *Awake five minutes and ordering me to get naked? You haven't changed.*

She rolled her eyes and headed into the bathroom. One of the best things about having a century-old farmhouse was the massive, claw-foot tubs. They were big enough for a man like Ste—*Savage* to sink way down and fully submerge in the warmth of a bath.

As the water level rose in a thundering rush, she eyed him up. "*And* you're bleeding." On his side, a mess of bloody bandaging hung loose. She picked at the tape to peel it free.

I'm fine. The wolf just got a lucky snap.

"And what's this?" She pointed at a second wound that looked nothing like an animal bite.

Bar fight fun before I came.

Fun? He put up a good front, but despite him playing the tough guy, he was a big fat faker. Now who was swaying and needed to rest? "I'll find something for you to wear while your clothes are washed and dried."

I'm fine, he signed. *Really.*

"You promised me no lies. Don't ruin it. My kid sister lives with me now. The last thing she needs is to see your junk airing out."

Leaning over the tub to the window ledge, she selected two bottles. After adding eucalyptus and lavender to the water, she fetched a couple fresh towels from the cupboard. She caught an eyeful as she returned and stopped dead.

She'd seen him naked dozens of times, but she'd never seen the evidence of his brutal life marring his skin. Where had all those scars come from?

He must have caught her intake of breath because he stiffened and scowled. *Hiding my scars would be a lie, right? This is me, as honest as I get.*

He held his arms out from his sides and gave her a half-turn. The ornate inkwork covering his skin did a lot to distract from his battle scars—that, and the impossible beauty of his body itself. She'd forgotten how incredibly fit the man was.

She looked at the scabby mess from the wolf attack and the bar fight and all the other evidence of violence. It hurt her to think how many times he'd suffered injury. Had he gotten all those in the past three years? Had he suffered alone?

"There are so many." She traced a six-inch ridge of buckled skin from his rib to the dip of his spine. "How can you endure this kind of brutality and remain a soldier?"

He shrugged. *Being a soldier isn't* what *I am—it's* who *I am, to the very marrow of my bones.*

She supposed some people were born to it. "Do they hurt you now?"

He shook his head.

Good. Her fingers continued to document his life's battles down his back and across his buttocks until he walked out of her reach. When he headed for the toilet and lifted the seat, she took the hint and gave him some privacy.

I stepped away from Hannah before I turned and took her to the bathroom floor. With my back to her, she hadn't witnessed how the warmth of her fingers brushing over my scars affected me. Thanks to the sensory trip down injury lane, my cock was up, hard, and aching for her. Thankfully, she took the hint and left. Now I just had to stand over the toilet and wait for things to settle down.

The good news—she still loved me. I saw it in her eyes when she looked me over and felt the air spark when we were in the same room together.

The bad news—the pain was there too, deep and raw. I did serious damage by leaving without explanation.

Once I flushed and washed my hands, I stepped into the massive tub. The water displaced with my weight and rose to bob against my chest. I'd never admit it, but a hot soak with the vapor of Hannah's flowery oils coming off the water was the closest thing to heaven I'd experienced in ages.

It beat slaying enemies. It beat drinking with my brothers-in-arms. The only thing it didn't beat was making love to Hannah. I hoped that option opened up to me again one day. There had always been sensual ease between us, and at least that remained intact. She watched me strip down with more than clinical interest.

I could work with that.

"Holy crapballs."

I opened my eyes and followed the exaltation to the girl in flannel PJs eyeing me from the doorway. I scanned her position, the height of the tub walls, and the distance between the doorway, and my exposed parts and pieces.

"Hannah finally gets laid. Thank you, baby Jesus. She's *soooo* uptight. She needs to work off some stress, you know? Maybe you do. You look like you're no stranger to stress. Nice ink, by the way. You're not from around here, right? So, where'd you come from? The city? North Highland, I'm guessing, amirite?"

I blinked up at the highly animated, mini-me version of Hannah. Same silky chestnut hair falling straight past her shoulders, same oval face and rich, chocolate eyes. Was this what she was like as a kid? It was hard to imagine her with this much life bubbling out.

Hannah was deeply changed by her mother leaving their family as a child, and I met her while she mourned her father. We didn't talk about her childhood much, but I knew she considered her father her only parent.

"You don't talk much, eh?"

I stretched my chin up and pointed to the scar left behind from my brother stripping me of my voice box and gods-given power of verbal persuasion.

"Sick. Did you get ganked in a gang fight?"

This kid was hilarious. She started moving in, and I held up my palm. The tub was deep. From across the bathroom, I had a bit of privacy. If she got any closer, she'd get an eyeful. I swept my fingers away in hopes she'd get the gist.

"Yeah, okay," she said, undeterred. "We'll talk in a bit. There's time. Snow day! Awesomeballs, right? 'Kay, so, I'll make pancakes. You like pancakes? Of course you do. *Everyone* likes pancakes. I put chocolate chips in them. You're not allergic, are you? 'Kay, so, twenty minutes?

Nah, you look wiped. How 'bout half an hour? I'll go tell Hannah the plan."

I gave her a thumbs up, as much to get her to leave as anything else. Scarring the kid sister wasn't likely to win me any points. With the silence renewed, I laid my head back, deciding whether to jump out and get dressed or enjoy a few more minutes.

Closing my eyes, I gave myself over to soaking.

"Is that a smile?" Hannah swept back into the master bath and closed the door. "Will wonders never cease."

I left the smile in place and my eyes closed. Raising my hands, I let the water rain down as I spoke. *My mysterious, tough-guy image is ruined forever. I met the sister. She's got energy to burn.*

"No kidding. She's great though, and I love her to bits. I didn't even know about her until I got the call from Tulsa Family Services."

I sat up and gave her my full attention. *What happened?*

"A couple of months after you left, my mother and her second husband were killed in a car accident. The placement decision was between me and a great aunt on her father's side. I won the lottery and inherited a ten-year-old. We've been fumbling to keep it together ever since."

I'm sure you're an amazing team. She's a cool kid.

Hannah's gaze narrowed. "I won't let you use Riley to make good with me."

Not what I was doing.

"Somehow, I doubt you see a chatty, pushy teenager as anything other than a pain in the ass."

Maybe my reputation as a badass asshole is overrated.

"Not by my experience." Anger tainted her voice, and the effect didn't suit her.

I can be more than that.

"I thought so, once upon a time. I won't make that mistake again."

I'm sorry. I fucked up and hate that I hurt you.

"You've said that."

And I'll keep saying it until you believe me.

"I believe you. It just doesn't change anything."

The regret in her eyes pierced me as if a dagger lanced my chest. Rising to my feet, I snagged the towel off the rack and stepped onto the cushy blue bathmat.

"What are you doing? You just got in there."

I patted the moisture from my arms, neck, and chest before wrapping my hips tight and tucking in the towel tail to keep things covered. *Riley is making me pancakes. Believe me or don't. I like the kid.*

"Don't hurt her. It won't end well for you."

I frowned, at the green plaid shirt and pink lamby pajama pants she'd brought for me to wear. Payback? I didn't give a shit. I would wear a tutu and heels if it got me closer to taming her anger. A warm drip slid down my side, and I reevaluated my drying procedures.

The two holes in my side were leaking a pale pink stain toward my towel. Freeing a few tissues, I blotted it off before I ruined her linens. *You got any gauze strips lying around?*

"Sorry. I don't patch many knife wounds. I've got some wraps I use on the horses."

The whirl of snow battering the bathroom window made that option less than ideal. Flashing there would be quick, but I just got all warm and cozy. *How about a feminine pad and an elastic tensor bandage?*

Her eyes widened. "If your machismo can take it, I can do that."

I chuckled, thinking about Mika patching up Bruin when their shit hit a year-and-a-half ago. *If the King of Weres can pull it off, no one will judge me too harshly. Of course, Bruin decapitates guys like dead-heading daisies. Still, I'll be good.*

She pulled a couple of plastic packages from under the vanity and set them on the countertop. "As long as you're good and I get to keep my head."

After she dabbed my side with yellow salve, I held the absorbent side of the pad in place while she wrapped things up. I tried not to focus on the rounds of her breasts pressed against my back as she reached around me and passed the length of bandage around and around my waist.

Tried. And failed.

I cleared my throat, and took the loose end of the tensor in one hand, the two metal clips in the other. Taking a leisurely stroll in the opposite direction of the bathroom, I avoided displaying massive tenting of my towel.

I stopped at the window and pretended the weather intrigued me. The polar vortex swirling around out in the barnyard slapped at the windows, and I gave thanks for the snow pinning us down for a bit. *The two wolves I took care of. Were they here because they knew you had the Alpha's mate? How did they find you?*

"They smelled that I had been to Jessop's farm, and followed. They were surprised to see that I had Myra."

Did you go inside the Alpha's farmhouse?

She closed her eyes against the memory and swallowed. "No. They were out front on the lawn. I didn't go close or touch them."

Did the two who attacked you make any calls or text the info back to anyone?

"Not that I know of. One was a wolf. The other, Carter, saw Myra, attacked me, and you know the rest."

The growl that vibrated in my chest was nothing I could control. Hannah had been mere seconds away from death, from me never making things right, from Riley waking up to an empty house and another family nightmare.

If Julian hadn't called Kobi . . . if I had stopped to grab my go-bag . . . any number of seemingly insignificant decisions would have wrought a devastating end. It fisted my guts and twisted tight. *The storm will erase your scent and keep the wolves at bay. Not even Weres would go out in this. We have a bit of time.*

"Good, I'll go out, check on Myra, and start chores."

I checked on the wolf before I crashed. She's deep in a healing sleep and will be out for hours if not days. The herd is fed, the horses bedded down. You're inside until dusk.

Hannah could stare a man down as well as any Talon Enforcer. It was damn impressive. "Believe it or not, bossy man, I can take care of you, get the morning chores done, *and* check on Myra, all by myself."

Scary that she thought so.

I admired her independence—always had—but she didn't know

39

shit about injured Weres. I propped my ass onto the edge of the bathroom vanity and backpedaled. *It would be best if you didn't get anywhere near the wolf, doc. A Were in a healing sleep is vulnerable and dangerously aggressive. I don't want you hurt.*

"Myra's my friend. She wouldn't—"

I pointed to a healed bite mark scarring my right hip. Then I pivoted, tugged the towel down my ass to show her the matching teeth punctures on my back.

"What happened?"

Cowbo—your boy, Waylon, got hurt bad in battle and I had to muscle him back to base. Weres can't always control their base animal. Wolves are known for it, some of the larger cat species are worse.

"There are other Were species?"

The surprise in her voice caught me off guard. Hadn't she thought about it? If Weres existed, why wouldn't there be other species? Maybe she didn't want to think about it. Maybe the truths of my world would be too much for her.

"You're not one . . ." she said, interrupting my mind-spiral. "I mean, you don't shift into an animal, do you?"

The idea intrigued her. I recognized the sexual glimmer in her eyes and smiled despite myself. *No, I'm a different kind of deadly altogether.*

She popped her brow and blushed. "You're not so tough. With a maxi wrapped to your hip and wearing only a towel, I bet I could take you."

In two quick steps, I pinned her to the linen closet door. Careful not to hit her broken wrist, I restrained her, rendering her helpless to move or struggle free.

She gasped, and I pressed my hips forward. The sexual glimmer sparked a flame. I kept her there, locked down in my clutches, and drew my tongue down the pulsing rhythm of her carotid artery. Fight or flight was real.

Her adrenaline pumped with feeling and, since she wasn't panicked, worked in my favor.

"Riley's cooking . . ." Her head dropped back, and I nipped the base of her throat. Gods, she tasted good. I missed having my mouth on her.

Bastard that I was, I recognized her hunger and took advantage. Wound like this, she'd be fast. I could ease her before her brain caught up and she pushed me away. Reveling in how the lush curves of her body accepted mine, I reached under her knit sweater and palmed the mound of her breast.

She gasped and pressed harder into my palm. This was happening. Hannah wanted it—I needed it. Making quick work of opening her jeans, I pulled them down her thighs.

She yanked one ankle free, and that was all I needed.

My bare knees hit the tiles, and my excitement drowned out the sound of the storm in my ears. I swung her freed leg over my shoulder and went for her core. Heaven. Teasing and nuzzling her simple cotton underwear, I blew hot kisses against her damp heat.

A gift. Being granted access to sweep my mouth over her fired every cell in my body. It was better than I remembered and more than I deserved. Playing. Priming. Promising. I met the feminine fragrance of her arousal and breathed deep, winding her up and feeding my soul.

Oh, fuck. Heat singed my balls so hot, I came. I groaned against Hannah's core and fought not to draw attention. It wasn't a wild explosion but a release so achingly sweet, I had to fight against the wave of dizziness that followed.

Thankfully, fighting was my superpower.

With my mouth still moving on her core, nothing would stop me from making amends. The damp cotton that kept me from my goal snapped in two, and my path was clear. It wasn't romance. It was raw need.

A need to taste her before I lost my mind.

A need to coat my throat with her essence.

A need to quench the raging thirst that had plagued me for three fucking years.

More than all that, it was a need to wash away the pain I caused and replace it with even one moment of blissful pleasure.

Craning my neck, I suckled the sensitive bud of her clit into my mouth and devoured. No sweet nuzzles—no butterfly-kiss bullshit. I licked and lapped like a wildcat given the gift of the finest cream.

"Oh, yes." She ground against my face and a fresh rush of nectar met my tongue. She tasted like honey and sunshine, and I groaned at the perfection. Her clit, tight and swollen, met my swiping tongue as she rode my mouth.

I slicked my fingers with a frenzied front to back in her moist channel. The pulsing grip of her core took hold the instant I slipped inside and another wave of dizziness hit.

"Yes," she hissed. She gripped my skull, pulling me harder to her core. Her reckless buck and grind had me so fucking wound, my vision fritzed. Such a greedy girl.

I fucked her in long, teasing strokes of fingers and tongue, and worked her to a throbbing passion. I knew her moods. And with her, this wild and panting, I pushed further.

With my fingers pressed deep inside her, I brushed my thumb over the tight flesh of her backside. I didn't enter. I didn't want to throw her out of the moment or start her mind. This was only about sensation. Playing. Teasing.

Hannah came apart with a throaty scream. I held her up as her legs quivered and her body convulsed. I lapped and swallowed. Her cream warmed my tongue and coated my throat. The gift of pleasuring her soothed my restless soul more than anything else ever could.

Panting, she stepped to the side and leaned against the edge of the counter. Cheeks flushed. Chest heaving. Hair tossed. Eyes heavy-lidded and sexy. So. Fucking. Beautiful.

I rose before her and raked the length of her hair down her sweater, my breath tight in my chest. *Thank you.*

She shook her head. "That was sex. Nothing more. It wasn't for you. It was for me."

Fair enough. I'd take the "just sex" train and ride it as long and hard as she let me. When she stilled, watching me, waiting for my reply, I nodded my understanding.

Just sex. Got it.

CHAPTER FOUR

*H*annah tidied the bathroom and hung the damp towels before getting changed and grabbing Savage's wet clothes. Her legs still trembled, and she needed to regroup. Sex with Savage always unraveled her. When he touched her like that—when he worshipped her body the way only he did, she was lost. The sensation was deceiving. The ecstasy didn't last. She learned that when he left her broken three years ago.

Dropping the basket of wet and dirty in front of the dryer, she took solace in the mundane motions of laundry. Simple tasks anchored her to reality.

Savage wasn't simple. He was the opposite of simple.

She didn't consider herself an overly impetuous woman but asking him to build a life with her on the ranch was by far the most reckless thing she'd ever done. She laid her heart on the line, and though she thought they had something extraordinary, he disappeared within hours and proved her wrong.

Why go down that road again?

He made his choice. The pain and embarrassment that speared her was good. She needed to keep it in her mind and heart to avoid making the same mistake again.

After checking the pockets of his jeans, she threw them into the washer with her load and tossed his shredded and bloody t-shirt in the trash.

She tried not to think about the wound on his side and headed out to the kitchen. Riley was busy destroying the kitchen as Savage knelt at the hearth on the far side of the open room, reviving the burned-out fire.

Chief bounded over to her and she ruffled his ears before heading over to start a pot of mocha latte coffee. "So, I heard you met Savage."

Riley looked up from the dough-splattered griddle and smiled. "Yup. He was nakey in your tub. Good going, Han. He's like ohmygod Olympic god ripped."

Hannah smiled and got down two mugs. "He'll be here for a day or two, helping me with a wolf problem. Are you okay with that?"

"Okay that there's a wolf problem I didn't know about? Umm, no, definitely not okay. Since when? Did they get in the barn? Is that why you went out last night? Geez, Hannah, you shoulda told me. You coulda got munched out there by yourself. Is that what happened to your arm?"

"Whisky Jack threw me and I landed badly on my arm."

"But Whisky threw you 'cause of a wolf, amirite?"

"Yes, but it turned out fine. The wolves caught me off guard, but Savage was there to help. He offered to watch over us for a bit, and I took him up on it. I don't want you uncomfortable with him in the house, though. I'll set him up in the barn if you are. This is *your* home, first and foremost."

Riley stacked another round of golden-brown discs into the warming bin and turned down the bacon. "I'm good. He's not much of a talker, but if he fights off wolves—so cool. That scar on his throat is righteous too. Oooh, do you think a wolf did that? I was thinking more like a Jack the Ripper scenario."

Hannah stopped pouring. "Riley, why do you think up stuff like that? Girls your age should be obsessing about boy bands and retro fashion trends, not the scars of strange men."

Riley faked a big yawn and headed to the table with two platters. "Breakfast is ready, dude."

Dude? Great. Of course Savage wouldn't put her on alert. She was a teenaged freak of nature and loved all things dark and dangerous. Honestly, that apple didn't fall far from the tree. She'd been the same at her age.

"Oh, I'm loving the pink jammie pants. Only a truly secure man could pull it off."

Hannah couldn't help but laugh. Riley was a kick. Nothing phased the kid. Putting Savage in pink was childish, sure, but it made her feel better, and he seemed determined to take whatever she dished him.

She read his comment and relayed the message. "He says everything looks and smells great. Thank you."

Savage had impeccable table manners.

She remembered that once they were elbow-deep in syrup and coffee. It always struck her as odd. Now, knowing a bit about his past, she was even more curious. Would his vow to answer her questions with full transparency still be in effect? Only one way to find out. "So, after your falling out with your brother, where did you live?"

Savage set down his cutlery and wiped his fingers on his napkin. He looked to her and she nodded that she would translate. *A man named Maximus Reign recruited me into a military group called the Talon. He is a highly-respected warrior and runs a sanctuary for misfit orphans where he trains them and gives them the skills they need to succeed.*

"Like Hogwarts?" Riley asked, adding another layer of syrup to her plate.

Savage seemed to consider that and then nodded. *Actually, yeah. A lot like Hogwarts.*

"So cool. What's it called? Can I look it up?"

He shook his head. *Sorry kid. Sworn to secrecy on that one. Besides, you'd never find it. Reign's adopted son, Julian, is a computer genius and makes sure nothing about us leaks into the real world.*

Hannah translated, and her sister looked like she might bug out completely. "Ri, I'm sure it's not as clandestine as all that. You're teasing her, aren't you?"

Savage frowned. *Nothing but the truth, remember? I swear. We're there, but nobody would ever know.*

"Can I go there if I'm with you?"

Yes, but that depends on your sister and whether or not I can fix what I fucked up.

Hannah didn't translate. She glared at him and shook her head. "No, sorry. You're stuck here."

Riley frowned. "That's not what he said. What'd he really say? How do you know sign language, anyway? Why didn't I know you knew? What else don't I know?"

Hannah finished her coffee and started stacking plates. "My best friend in high school developed a brain tumor in the summer before our senior year. About six months in, they operated, but whether it was taking the tumor or the treatments afterward, she became deaf afterward. In the weeks it took for her to recover her strength, we spent our time learning to sign."

Did she live, though? Savage asked. *Healthy after that?*

Hannah nodded. "Yeah, she got married to a pilot and moved to Arizona. Last I heard, they had three kids."

"That's nice," Riley said, starting the rinse and load for the dishwasher. "Is that where you got the Arizona State sweatshirt you wear? From her?"

"That's where." Between the three of them, it didn't take long to clean up and get things squared away. "Okay, I'm heading to the barn. Savage can help me with your chores this morning, Ri."

"Woohoo, thanks, Sav. Can I call you Sav?"

Savage nodded and signed.

"He said you're welcome to call him that. All his closest friends do."

"Sweet. I knew it. I've got a sixth-sense about things like that. So, no chores. Maybe I'll—"

"Work on that group project that's due on the twelfth."

Riley groaned. "What part of 'group' don't you get? We're snowed in, and snow days are days off. Besides, townies sleep in. They don't have to do morning chores before school."

Hannah headed down the hall and grabbed her coat. "There's this thing called Skype. You know, you're on it all the time. It can be used for good as well as evil. Have your shower, do what you can on your own, and then call your friends after ten. They'll survive."

I followed tight on Hannah's nine, blocking the wind the best I could. Futile effort. The stormfront blew in from the north, straight across the acreage, the gusts hitting the outbuildings and swirling like a snowmageddon from every direction. Icy pellets pummeled our faces as we sank knee-deep in fresh snow with every step.

As much as I hated it, the violence of the storm was the only thing buying me time to spend with Hannah before shit hit. I couldn't complain. Except, we weren't getting far, and Hannah winced every time she corrected her balance and stiffened her broken wrist.

After what seemed like ten minutes trying to wade across the yard, I gave up. Wrapping my arms around her, I Flashed us to the tack room of the barn. It was a risk, sure, but I didn't have the luxury of time to wait for my openings when she didn't want to talk about anything serious.

I held her close while she adjusted to her warped reality. Flashing took getting used to. The first few times, it felt like a buzzsaw whirled in your head, and ants crawled on your skin.

She recovered too soon for my liking and shook me off. Pulling back, she stumbled out into the corridor. "What the . . . How'd we get here? Did I black out?"

I brought you here with my powers. I wasn't lying, doc. Hogwarts, remember? My world is very different than yours. Weres and magic are only the tip of the iceberg.

Her horse reached its head over his stall door and gave her an insistent shove. She steadied herself and scrubbed its brow. "Do it again. I want to see. Go to the end of the corridor and back."

I Flashed the fifty feet to the far end of the corridor and then back. Materializing a good ten feet away. I gave her enough space that I hoped she wouldn't feel threatened.

I am a soldier for a man named Castian. He is the god of the Fae and bestows the ability to travel by materializing and dematerializing at will to his senior officers. We call it Flashing. I stood, palms up and open to her. Letting the truth of my words shine through, I waited.

Her brow tightened, as if she was working through things. "That's how you got to me so quickly despite the weather? When I called Waylon last night."

I nodded.

"And when you say *Fae,* you mean witches and sprights and fairies and such?"

Yes, things of that nature. Weres are only one species in my world. I watched her closely, lips apart, breath shallow and quick. Did she think me crazy? Likely not. By her reaction, she was simply processing.

"I don't fit into your world. That's why you left me?"

Despite wanting to pull her against my chest and wrap her in a tight embrace, I forced myself to keep my distance and keep my hands moving. *I admit, I didn't want to make you choose between a life you love and one you have no understanding of, but no. There was a war in my world when I left you, doc. My brother was behind it. He killed innocent people to fuel his ambitions. I left because it was my duty to stop him.*

When she said nothing, I continued. *When you asked me to commit to you and this life, I wanted to accept—too much. How could I live with myself if I ignored my oath to right his wrongs? I wanted to stay with you more than anything, but my wants didn't factor in. My brother had to be stopped. No one knew who he was and what motivated him better than I did. He was a vile, deplorable male.*

She stepped away from her horse's constant nuzzling. I couldn't tell if her annoyance stemmed from him or me. Her boots shuffled on the concrete floor, drawing her forward. "Was? This war—it's over now?"

Yeah, a few months ago.

"Months?" She stopped her approach. "If that was the reason you left why not come tell me right away? You're here now because I called Waylon for help. If I hadn't, you'd still be getting into drunken bar fights and living it up."

Was angry better or worse than disillusioned? I certainly wasn't living it up. I hadn't been living at all over the past three years. I'd been little more than existing as a miserable, warrior zombie going through the motions.

I wanted to come sooner. I . . . I was afraid you wouldn't take me back. Somehow, leaving the possibility out there seemed better than a final no.

She laughed, but it was hard and cold. "You expect me to believe that you're a coward? After everything you are and do, you're saying you were afraid to face me? I don't buy it."

My hope sank. *I'm sorry. I was focused for so long, that once Abaddon was no longer a factor, I was lost. I didn't know who I was or what I could offer you or my realm or even myself. I've been fucked up.*

The disappointment in her eyes hollowed me out.

The wild bellowing of upset cattle broke the tension and brought me up short. Something, or someone, had the herd riled up. I ushered Hannah back inside the tack room and backed out. *Wait here and lock the door.*

"It's nothing," she snapped. "Cattle do that all the time. The weather—"

I get that you don't trust me but for once, do as I say.

Her glare grew hot and hard. "I trust you."

Bullshit.

"Not with my heart, but I trust you with my life."

I took the hit, and with a bazooka-sized hole hollowing my chest, pointed a warning finger. *Stay here.*

Hannah hated being bossed around, but the sudden surge of violence in Savage's dark eyes convinced her not to argue. She was out of her depths. Magic. Evil twins. God of the Fae. She *clicked* the latch behind him and grabbed some saddle oil and a cloth. The cattle being riled was nothing, she was almost sure. Savage had a hero complex a mile wide. If he thought danger abounded, he needed to handle it. This was the real him. Not a Marine. Not a farmhand. Savage was a senior soldier in the service of the God of the Fae.

She couldn't wrap her mind around that.

If he hadn't Flashed her into the barn and then shown her again how it worked, she'd call him delusional and show him the door. She'd seen people turn into wolves and felt the magic of his transport tingle beneath her skin.

She couldn't explain that away.

Still, if they were under attack, she wasn't about to stay locked in a tack room while he defended everything she held dear. Striding over to the corner of the room, she unlocked the gun locker and pulled out her daddy's rifle. Bullets probably worked better on Weres than shot pellets, right?

She thought so.

Loading up, she filled her pockets with extra rounds and headed toward the door. If wolves were there, they were after Myra. She wasn't abandoning her neighbor without one heck of a fight.

I paused outside the tack room door until I heard Hannah *click* the lock on the other side of the slab. After laying it out for her, there was no way I would let Weres or cattle or flying pigs interrupt our forward momentum. She would sort through the info I gave her, and she'd forgive me. She had to. It was the only option.

Stalking up the corridor, I couldn't believe I was about to fight a pack of angry wolves wearing pink pajama pants with cute little lambs on them. At least I had my dagger sheathed to my thigh . . . and they wouldn't live to tell the tale. Surveying the goings-on in the main barn, I didn't see anyone from my position back from the entrance.

If I hadn't spent months with the cattle that first time, I wouldn't be so sure trouble brewed. But, from the direction the cows stared and how they huddled away, I knew where the intruders were as clear as if I had a scope in the next room.

Trusting in the bovine intel, I outed my guns and Flashed into the opposite corner of the holding room.

One. Two. Three. Back to Hannah and me.

The right cross to my jaw came out of nowhere and hurt like a motherfucker. As my lights flickered, I gave the Were with the concrete fists credit. Distracted as I was, I hadn't seen that coming, and the guy had a first-rate punch. My head rang as if I clocked it against a bell.

I spit blood. The metallic gob of scarlet splashed the jacket of my attacker as the asshole closed in for hand-to-hand. Impatient to get back to Hannah, I blocked the swing, steeled my fists, and went to town.

The startled look of surprise made me smile. Why did pack Weres always think themselves the top of the food chain? They never realized there were bigger, badder things in the realms than them.

I would've toyed with him longer, but with Hannah isolated and Riley alone in the house, I had to lock things down. Man, my dead body hiding spot was about to get crowded. Good thing two hundred cattle produced a lot of fresh shit every day.

When my foe hit the pitted concrete floor, I brushed myself off and Flashed back to the tack room—which was empty. No signs of forced entry and the gun safe was hanging open. *Fuuuuck.*

Why couldn't she ever do what she was told?

Throwing my molecules to the wind, I started a frantic search. Would she go for Myra or Riley? I honestly couldn't guess. The Hannah of three years ago had been driven and independent, but the woman I was dealing with now was downright obstinate.

We needed to get to know one another again.

A shot fired in the distance and my bowels practically liquefied. As I followed the sound, a second shot rang off, hard on its heels. Drive shed.

I materialized in time to tackle Hannah out of the way as a huge gray wolf lunged from behind. When it rounded hard and came back, I unsheathed my dagger and met it head-on. The wolf's skull fought my blade for a half-second before I plunged straight into its head.

Hannah screamed and I blew the head off the man grabbing at her, bits of brain and gray matter detonating like a bomb in every direction. Before another one came at us, I clutched Hannah to my chest, and Flashed straight inside the farmhouse. *Safeguard your sister. I've fucking got this.*

I Flashed back into the fray, the image of Hannah standing in the living room, pissed and glaring, making me smile. *Women.*

CHAPTER FIVE

en. Hannah turned to Riley staring up at her from her homework set out on the dining room table. She was in no mood. She dropped the barrel of the gun and stomped down the front hall to make sure the front door was still locked. Not that it would make a lick of difference. Werewolves were strong enough to come straight through the solid walnut.

Back in the living room, Riley was still staring. "Huh, first time for everything, eh? You speechless?"

"How? You poofed there and then, poof, he was gone."

"Hogwarts, remember?"

Riley's eyes widened even more. "Holy shit. No way."

"Language, missy." Hannah emptied some ammunition from her coat pocket and set things up on the island counter. After reloading, she laid the gun down and pointed. "Don't touch that gun. You don't know how to use it, and you'll have better luck throwing things and running, got it?"

"Running from what?" she said, dropping her pencil and abandoning her project. "What's that in your hair?"

"Wolf brains."

"And you think they're going to get into the hou—" A bizarre expression clouded her kid sister's face before she broke into a wild grin. "Werewolves, amirite? All those hot, buff guys in town are Werewolves. Jed. Matt. Wayne. Bentley in chemistry class. Yeah, he's gotta be. Ohmigod, ohmigod, this is amazing."

"Reevaluate your definition of amazing, Ri. It's deadly and dangerous. You can't say anything, or they'll kill you."

Riley searched the room and grabbed a bronze rodeo trophy off the mantel. She tested the weight of the thing in her hand, looking more excited than scared. "Did you tell? Is that why they're after you?"

Savage Flashed into their midst, carrying a gold and caramel wolf in his arms. He laid her in front of the fire and patted Chief's head as the dog inched forward to investigate. *The fight took out the heat lamps in the drive shed, and her scent would spook the livestock. She's not getting any better. I'll have to phone a friend.*

Riley looked at the wolf curled up, and her mouth fell open. "Who's that? Do you know?"

"It's Myra. I found her in the creek last night. When I brought her home, I offended the other wolves." Hannah waved away the look of censure Savage speared her with and shrugged. "The jig was up when you Flashed us in right in front of her. We're in this now. Like it or not."

By the scowl on his face and the tightness of his brow, she guessed that was a big "not". *I'll be back. I gotta get rid of the bodies and bury their scents. I'm stashing them under the manure pile, by the way.*

"Are we in the clear for now?"

He shrugged. *Depends if they were here scouting or if they knew about Myra. I hate bringing her inside but didn't think you'd forgive me if I let her die in the cold.*

"No. I wouldn't."

Hannah called Chief away from Myra and took off her coat. Her pants were wet from plodding through the drifts to the barn, and she was sweating and chilled from fighting. Savage would be even worse after burying the dead.

"So, what now?" Riley asked. "Once a pack cites you for elimination, you're toast. We'll be on the run now, unless we can get the Alpha to call things off."

"What?" Hannah filled the kettle and stared. "You're making that up."

"No. I read Mercy Thompson, thank you very much. She's always dealing with shit like this with Adam and his pack."

Hannah let the curse slide, under the circumstance. "Sad news there, Ri. Jessop was the Alpha and Jed was next up. I found them both dead right before I found Myra."

"Oh no." Riley slumped back into a chair. "Then what do we do?"

The kettle clicked off, and Hannah tossed in two bags and filled the teapot. She used the last of the boiled water to make a hot chocolate for Riley. "Savage is here to keep us safe. He's a Fae soldier who deals with this stuff all the time. I don't want you afraid—cautious, yes —but not afraid."

"You knew him before last night, though, didn't you? He's like an old boyfriend or something, amirite?"

She handed Riley her mug and sighed. "That's none of your business, nosy girl. Focus on what's happening now. We might have to pull up roots until things settle down."

Riley swallowed, looking all business. "You better call Tandy and tell him he might have to run the farm for a bit."

Hannah pulled out her phone and called up his number. "Good idea. Take your hot chocolate to your room and pack a bag. Keep it light and just essentials."

"A go-bag, got it." Riley got moving, the smile on her face so inappropriate. Before she ducked into the hall, she turned back. "Hey, do you think if things don't settle here that I could go to Savage's Hogwarts school. How cool would that be, amirite?"

Hannah groaned and went to retrieve the bottle of acetaminophen from the coffee table. She tipped a bunch onto the island next to her tea and her rifle and, after swallowing three, prayed either her arm or her head would stop throbbing.

Both would be better, but she didn't hold out much hope.

She had a sinking feeling in the pit of her stomach that things would get worse before they got better.

~

I buried the last wolf and left the shovel stuck in the shit pile. Odds were good I'd be back there again soon, so no need to go Martha Stewart and put things away. Stepping off the mound, I tightened the collar of my leather jacket, wiped my boots clean on the snow, and Flashed into the front hallway of the farmhouse.

After unbuckling the metal snaps of my shitkickers, I pulled my sweat-soaked feet from my boots. Normally, I'd leave them on in case another surge of hostility hit, but I was sure we had time to regroup and was chilled to the bone.

Hot from physical exertions, but at the same time, freezing and shivering in the torn, wet, pink flannel pants, I felt like a heap of shitty contradictions.

Riley handed me a hot mug the second I emerged into the living space. "I've got my go-bag packed and put together some of Chief's food and his favorite squeaker toy. Hannah said we might have to bug out."

I tossed my gloves over the heat register and sipped at the heated edge of the ceramic mug. I wasn't a tea drinker, but at that moment, it was hot, and it was kind of Riley, so I drank it down with a nod of thanks.

"FYI, Hannah's taking a shower. I think you should get in there before she uses all the hot water. She's got it bad for you, you know? I can tell. Anyway, you should go. I'll be fine out here, with my head-phones in and my music on. Maybe you should leave me a gun. I'll only interrupt if there's an emergency . . . just sayin'."

Gods, she looked so much like her older sister. I'd bet if we got out the albums, I wouldn't be able to tell them apart without using the backgrounds to sleuth things out. Reaching over the chaos of home-work and school supplies, I snagged a pencil and got writing.

1. *No gun. You aren't trained, and stats prove you're more likely to get disarmed and shot, than save yourself.*
2. *Headphones out. Stay alert to your surroundings and take cues from Chief. He'll sense an intruder before you will.*
3. *Stay away from the wolf. She's in a healing sleep and Weres are vicious and dangerous when vulnerable.*
4. *If you need anything—even if you just get the creeps—interrupt. If you're in trouble, run right in without second thought. Nothing is more important than your safety, got it?*

I waited for her to finish reading and then held out a fist for a bump. She didn't hesitate. She even made the explosion noise and spread her fingers like Coal did when I bumped with him.

Chuckling, I took the wingman advice of the teenager and headed through Hannah's bedroom to the large en suite bath. I wasn't sure if the unlocked door was an invitation or simply her habit, but I preferred to think of it as a welcome.

Standing with my back to the bathroom door, I stripped down and stalled out. Was this too much too soon? Not for me. Gods, after seeing her face death twice in twenty-four hours, I needed her with everything in me. I longed to linger at her lips. Ached to wrap myself around her. Burned to lose myself inside her heat while her body pulsed and pulled and the world melted away.

One look at her and I was hard as granite and hungry.

With her eyes closed against the spray, the impish grin on her face had me wondering what filled her mind. Could it be me? Maybe? Hopefully? Was I right thinking Hannah still loved me? I prayed so.

Hannah had full ownership of everything in me, and I wanted her to take advantage. The "just sex" offer was great, and would soothe the most ragged of needs, but I wanted more.

I wanted it all. Wrapped up. Locked down. Everything.

But what if she truly, deep down, didn't want that? What if I was deluding myself? I faced the strongest, most deadly situations imaginable, but I had never been as afraid to act as I was at that moment.

Please, doc. Love me back.

Taking the header into freefall, I opened the glass door and closed us in together. Hannah peeked out of one eye, saw it was me, and went back to worshipping the hot spray as if she'd known I would come all along.

With my heart hammering, I pressed behind her and slid my hands over the rise and falls of her slick, wet body. Thankful for even this, I kissed the back of her shoulder and got reacquainted.

Unlike the massive antique tub, the shower was a few decades more modern and confining. The tight dimensions were a plus. No matter how she turned or shifted, there was no getting away from one another. I remained within easy reaching distance of one body part or another.

With a smile on my face, I wrapped one arm under her breasts and sent the other lazily down her thigh. She arched against my chest, the crack of her ass hugging the length of my cock. "I'm having trouble washing my hair with my wrist. Would you mind?"

Hells to the no.

Reaching around her, I snagged the pretty bottle of organic shampoo and squeezed a blue puddle into the palm of my hand. After rubbing it into a lather, I started at the line of her scalp and worked back to the lengths of dark chestnut.

Heaven. Seriously.

My breath locked in my lungs as I struggled not to tear up. Yep, I was being stripped down to a total Nancy girl by my emotions. I didn't give a shit. Being able to service her in some way made things so much easier on my end. As a task-oriented male, give me a job, and it'll get done.

With gentle fingers, I massaged her scalp and lathered the wet fall of hair down her back. When things were solidly taken care of, I turned her to face me to rinse and repeat. Using my thumbs at the top of her forehead, I ensured no soapy water got into her eyes. I shifted her one step closer to get the water to fall off the back of her head.

The change in position had us rubbing front-to-front.

A mewling sound escaped Hannah's throat, and I took the cue. Her mouth met mine, hot and inviting, and the rest of her body followed close behind. Hands seeking. Arms tightening. With our wet skin, the heat and friction of gliding against each other had me trembling with anticipation.

Hannah was right there with me.

A sure hold claimed my cock and my knees almost buckled. I dropped my head back and swallowed, waiting for my vision to clear. She tightened her grip and stroked tip to balls and back again.

After a minute or two, I squeezed her hand and tugged for her to release. I wouldn't last if she kept that up. It had been too long, and I wanted this too much.

"It's fine," she said, refusing to be derailed. "Let me take the edge off for you. It's been one heck of a tough day and you've done a lot for me."

There was no arguing with Hannah. Who was I kidding? I didn't want to argue. Pressing one hand to the tile wall to keep from falling, I slid the other under her jaw to reclaim her kiss. The sting building at the base of my sac had me cursing the ecstasy of her touch.

I wanted this to last. Forever.

"I wish I had two good hands for this. You're bigger than I remember," she breathed against my lips. She rocked me with a slow up and down, squeezing almost enough to make me beg.

Fuck almost. *More*. Being mute sucked.

I tilted my hips, pressing harder into her grip. She got the message and got rough. My length slid in her fist, silky sheath over marble column. Her nails scraped the tender flesh with each stroke, drawing me ever closer to plummeting.

When she reached the top of the next stroke, she flicked her thumb through the slit of my crown. Lightning shot a hot flame from the base of my spine to the nape of my neck. Tiny electrical shocks ignited under my skin.

My breath caught. Muscles tensed. *Oh, gods . . . yes.*

Hot streams spewed onto my abs, her hand, my thigh. Over and over, the pleasure racked me. Her hand slicked with cum, my body convulsing as I panted through it.

This was more than sex. For me, anyway. I was hers. She was mine. It was that simple.

When things settled down, I turned her toward the spray and washed her off. The nip to the tender column of her neck served as my thanks, and she got the message because she smiled over her shoulder and winked.

With my semi-hard cock nestled along the crease of her ass, I reached for the conditioner. I had a job to do, and I'd be damned if I neglected my duty. Back on track, regardless of the tremble in my legs, I resumed the lather and massage and marveled at how her curves glistened under the spray.

Finished with the second stage of hair care, I rinsed things clean, and shut off the water. I wanted her beneath me—desperately—but also wanted to allow her to set the pace.

When I opened things up and leaned out to grab a towel, she stroked me from breast to thigh and back again.

Yeah, doc. Keep that up.

I wrapped her in the towel and, inch by delicious inch, dried her off. She arched to my ministrations, surging against my touch. The vibration burning inside me rose with every brush of her skin, every drip collected.

My love for Hannah called out to the darkest part of me. Warmed the icy chill. Demanded I pleasure her. Mark her. Claim her. If I were a Were, I'd say my animal side claimed her as my mate. I was bonded.

Lifting her against my chest, I turned toward the bedroom.

"No," she said, wriggling to get down. "Not in my bed. We're not that anymore."

Disappointment hit hard. I granted her freedom and stepped back, using the edge of the tub to keep me upright.

She folded the mile of terry I used to dry her and set it to hang over the edge of the countertop of the bathroom vanity. "You destroyed me when you left. I won't go through that again."

I held my expression blank even as her words pierced my cold, dark heart. *I'm sorry*, I signed, but she wasn't looking, and I knew the evasion was intentional.

Facing the vanity, she opened the center drawer and pulled out a row of condoms and the coconut massage oil she always liked. "Just sex."

Right. What I took as a win before, now hollowed me out. If I was a stronger man, my pride might have told me to walk away. I wasn't. I couldn't. I needed her. I loved her.

Surely, I could prove that to her more each time we connected. Right? It wasn't over. It wasn't hopeless, was it? Dropping the towel from my hips, I stepped in behind her.

When she bent forward and rested her elbows on the counter, my heart stumbled behind my battered ribs. She didn't want me looking into her eyes. She didn't want me to creep behind her defenses.

Folding myself over her, I drew my tongue down the long line of her spine. The howl of the wind outside voiced my pain and, at the same time, was music to my ears.

As long as winter battled like a vengeful fury out there, we could take our time in here. Reaching across the counter, I picked up the massage oil and got things started.

With Hannah propped up on her elbows, I reached between her belly and the towel. The hanging weights of her breasts fit my hands perfectly, and the glide of the oil had my balls tingling. I gave each side a gentle squeeze, twisting the tightened buds of her nipples as I worked my way down her spine with my mouth.

"You always know how to work my body," she said, her hips swaying against my erection.

That's because I love you, I thought. *Because your body is mine to love, and bring to new heights.*

Working her with both my mouth and my hands, I worshipped her down to her tailbone. The throaty sounds she made when she was sexually impatient hadn't changed.

I wouldn't be rushed.

Gripping her hips, I bit the round of her ass hard enough to make her gasp. I knew the sounds she made and that one—the catch, the breathy hiss—yeah, that one put her squarely where I wanted her.

I smiled at the teeth marks pinking her tanned flesh and kissed the sting away. Her heated gaze met mine in the mirror, and I fought to keep things casual. If playing her game was my only access pass, I'd pretend this didn't mean everything to me. But it did.

The condom wrapper ripped between my teeth, and I tossed the empty foil. Once I was gloved for love, I gripped my throbbing length and played in her heat, slicking, teasing, probing. Notched at her entrance, I didn't push inside.

Her rejection hurt, and I was petty enough to want her to suffer at least a little frustration before I caved and gave her everything she wanted.

Hannah growled and pushed back. I countered and pulled my hips. She glared at me in the mirror, and I arched a brow. I wasn't one for games, but that didn't mean I didn't know how.

"Really? You're playing hard to get?"

I shrugged, pressing against her opening enough to start to breach. The gasp that escaped her lips had me pulsing. She must have felt it because she dropped her face to the towel and groaned.

Yeah, we were both stubborn enough that this standoff could last all afternoon. But really, what fun would that be?

The next time she pushed back, I let her take what she wanted. I didn't get in far. We'd always been a tight fit, but her sex would accept me as soon as I treated her right.

With one hand gripping her hip, I wrapped the other around to find that magic button of hers.

Hannah dropped to the counter and groaned at the injustice. Hot, panting, and so wound up she might explode with sexual frustration, she waved her tail in the air like a bitch in heat. She'd be embarrassed if it wasn't him, but Savage had always had this effect on her. Part of her hated it. A bigger part of her loved it. Craved it. Totally got off on it.

Her body had always been responsive to his touch.

He rubbed over her clit and continued to ease in and pull out. The

friction of fill and retreat incredible. It drove her to madness. "Please .
. . yes, more."

He grabbed the massage oil again and drizzled it down the base of
her spine. What was he— "Oh mercy."

That bad-boy thumb was back and playing. She never thought
she'd like something like that, had never entertained the idea of anal
play with any other man, but with Savage, she did, and he knew she
did. Her release built inside her, the throbbing wanton taking control.

She widened her stance and locked her knees. It had been ages
since she'd had great sex. No way she was ruining this by collapsing to
the bathroom floor. Whatever he was giving, she was taking. Even if—

"Ohmigoodness." She pushed back, his thumb breaching her backside as his erection pushed fully inside her sex. The animalistic growl
behind her triggered a rush of silk heat between her thighs.

The dual penetration was nothing short of invasive. Too much.
Not enough. The moisture it triggered gave him the glide to really
started moving.

Savage released her clit and gripped her hip, leveraging his hold to
pump harder. Faster. Bracing herself with her good hand pressed
against the mirror, she looked back and watched him take her. The
man was possessed, the feral look in his eyes as he focused on her was
waaaay too intense.

She closed her eyes as he rode her hips hard into the edge of the
counter. She didn't care, meeting every stroke with a groan of pleasure. The thrust and retreat, with the pressure of his invading thumb
had her flying beyond any discomfort she might feel. "Yes. Hard.
More. I can take more."

She dropped her head to the towel, her whole body on fire with
the ache for him. More thumb. More pounding. More Savage. The
slap of flesh to flesh echoed in her ears. The steamy air smelled of
coconut, sex, and the mixture of their scents. It was an aphrodisiac,
heady and addictive.

It was Savage.

Her world fractured and she blew apart. Light exploded behind
closed eyes as she screamed his name and cried out a string of

nonsense. She screamed for him again, another wave of agonizing pleasure trampling the first.

His grip grew bruising, his thrusts hard enough she'd swear he might break through her womb. His breathing caught in rough, bursting pants. And then he stiffened.

Behind her, his hips locked and she opened her eyes to watch him lose control. And he did.

The man who stood behind her was not the man she'd known three years ago. This man was wilder. Far more dangerous. Savage's head dropped back as he screamed in silent triumph. Long muscles stood out on his throat, his pulse pounding in the stretched veins of his neck.

It was beautiful, and at the same time—terrifying.

And then he collapsed to the floor in a dead faint.

CHAPTER SIX

I woke to the soft sawing snore of Chief on the end of the bed, and a silent world beyond. Not silent, as in lacking noise, but a vacuumed hush hanging over the outdoors that swallowed all the usual sounds of barnyard and beyond. The storm had ended, or moved off, cocooning the farm beneath a wooly blanket of insulating snow.

Shit. How long ago had that happened? I grabbed the edge of the blankets and was about to vault out of Hannah's bed when I saw Riley crossing the room.

"Hey, you're awake." Focused as she was on the tray she carried, the kid didn't seem to notice me covering things up on the quick. "Hannah's homemade soup for the sicky."

Riley made it all the way to the bed without spilling, and I propped myself up to accept the tray.

Where's your sister?

She watched my hands and frowned. "Sorry. Do you want Hannah?"

I nodded and gave her a thumbs up.

"Cool. I'll get her. Feel better, okay? And eat your soup. It's good, and good for you."

Lifting the spoon to my mouth, I made like I would chow down. When she left, I shifted the tray to the bedside table, flipped back the covers, and was up, searching for something to wear.

"Huh, Riley failed to mention that you were streaking around my room naked. I hope this happened *after* she came to get me. Impressionable teenagers and all."

I straightened from my search for clothes on the top of her dresser and frowned. *Where are my pants? I need my guns and my phone. How long was I out?*

Damn. My whole body ached. And shivered. And ached.

Hannah's fingers were cold on my hips as she steered me back toward the bed. "You push yourself too hard and regard yourself too little."

Probably. I shook my head—mistake. With my balance off, I tilted heavily to one side. I gave her credit. Hannah fought to keep me on my feet and won the battle. She'd muscled horses and cattle her whole life, and knew how to stand her ground against an overwhelming force.

My hard body pressed against her soft curves and I wished, once again, that this reunion had taken a different path. I wanted to be naked in her bed, just not like this.

"You collapsed on the bathroom floor a couple of hours ago. About twenty minutes later, you roused enough to help me get you to the bed. Your body needs rest, tough guy. Let's get you back there before you face-plant a second time."

She gave me a shove, and I dropped like a felled tree. So much for my mighty muscles. I was helpless. Thankfully, I threw the sheets back when I got up. There was no way she could lift me to get them freed from under my ass if I hadn't.

Pulling the blankets to cover things up, I cursed the damned fever. Hannah's care was incredible but now was not the time. Laying there with my eyes closed, I never wanted to move . . . but I had to.

With the storm over, the wolves would realize they were down eight men and start looking. I needed to stay alert and protect Hannah and her sister.

A hand brushed over my chest, and I winced. "Sorry. Is your skin too achy?"

There she was, set up with warm water and a face cloth. I couldn't believe I was nixing a sponge bath, but such was my life. I frowned and raised my hands. *Can I get a do-over once I feel better?*

Hannah's soft chuckle was all the medicine I needed. "Once you're better, I expect you out of my bed. This is only about you burnin' up. I took pity on your weakened state and knew I couldn't get you to a spare room."

Yeah, maneuvering my almost two-hundred-and-seventy-pound body down the hall to one of the empty guest bedrooms would've been a chore. I tried not to think about the times we'd shared in this bed.

Honestly, I never thought I'd be back.

It sucked that it wasn't as her lover, but whatevs. Incapacitated by fever gave me an in. Despite wanting to pull Hannah over my chest and sink into the sheets for the next two days, duty called. *Help me get dressed. I need my clothes. Please. We're running out of time.*

"You're in no shape to take on anything but rest."

That doesn't work for me.

She squeezed my arm and smiled. Her eyes were clouded with worry, and I knew she was fronting on my behalf. "It looks like you've lost the upper hand, soldier."

Hannah, seriously, I gotta get dressed and ready.

"No clothes, you're burning up as it is. Here, let me get these on you."

She took a pair of socks and pulled them over my feet. When the lumpy soles hit my arches, I screwed up my face and looked at her. *What the hell is in there?*

"Chopped onions."

Why?

"My gran always put cut onions in our socks when we were sick. It draws the germs and impurities out of your system. Here, drink this."

The brown concoction smelled like rotting assholes—hard pass. *I can't take anything. Don't you get it? Wolves will come. I need to defend you.*

The roll of her eyes gave me hope she was done arguing. Ha! Nope. She grabbed a blue and gold tin and twisted off the lid. "You're in no shape to do anything but recuperate. When are you expecting the trouble?"

Any time now. The storm was the only thing holding off their search. It won't take them long to track Myra here now.

Hannah rubbed a thick, menthol salve on my neck and chest, and swiped a finger under my nose. Cold on my skin, I shook the bed as another wracking shiver took me. *Is this cruel payback for my past transgressions?*

Her smile fell. "This is me helping you, despite them."

The hurt swimming in those big brown eyes pegged me in the chest. I gripped her wrist as she moved to pull away. *I'm sorry,* I mouthed, not letting her escape. *I should have said yes. Ask me again.*

She blinked, her expression going blank. Collecting the soup tray, she shifted it to the dresser. "Rest now. Riley and I will hold down the fort."

Wait. My guns and my phone. Hannah retrieved my belongings. I checked my Glocks, set them within reach, and called up the contacts list on my phone. I couldn't defend Hannah like this. Cowboy's pack could arrive at any time.

I needed reinforcements.

I hit send as the last ounce of energy evaporated. There were few people I trusted to watch over what was mine, but in this sitch, only one to call on.

I closed my eyes, the scent of Hannah engulfing me. Sprawling lifeless in her sheets wasn't all bad, especially with the image of her playing Florence Nightingale with the sponge bath etched into my memory.

If I died here, at least I'd die happy. My only regret would be that I let Hannah down.

Again.

~

Hannah shut the bedroom door and hurried back to check on Riley and Myra. The panic in Savage's eyes rattled her. They were in serious trouble and despite him thinking himself invincible, he wasn't up to the task of protecting them at the moment.

A knock sounded at the door and Chief barked, racing down the front hall. His nails clicked on the wood floor, and her heart raced in time with the beat.

Riley looked up from the table and grabbed the trophy. "Is it the wolves? Are they here?"

"I think so." Hannah couldn't see how anyone else could've made it through the aftermath of the snowstorm. The roads would be closed for hours. She grabbed her gun off the coffee table and headed to the door. Before she went down the hall, she signaled for her sister to get to the corner. "If I tell you, run into the bedroom. Savage has his guns."

"What about you?"

Hannah shook her head. "Do what you're told."

"Hello?" a woman said from the front porch. "Hannah? I got a text from Savage, asking me to join him here ASAP. Is everything all right? May I come in?"

Hannah's head hurt. Savage texted someone one minute ago. This Flashing stuff boggled her brain. Still, if he wanted her here, he had a reason.

The metal of the chain slid in its channel as she unlocked the door. The woman on her snow-covered porch stood tall and stunning—a full-figured redhead with piercing, emerald green eyes met her scrutinizing gaze with an easy smile.

"Hi, Hannah, I'm Jade. It's lovely to meet you."

Hannah looked down at her Colt, aimed and loaded, and felt heat creep across her cheeks. "Sorry."

Jade shrugged. "Better to be safe. Besides, if Sav's calling in reinforcements, you must've had quite a wild twenty-four hours. He asked me to secure you, your sister, and Cowboy's mother?"

"You know Waylon too?"

Jade smiled, unzipped her coat, and slid it off her shoulders.

69

"Know him and love him, yes. He's been part of my family since you saved him, and he needed a home. Thank you for that, by the way."

It warmed her to know that not everyone Waylon hung around with looked like an escaped convict and got into bar fights for fun. Though, she had a feeling that despite Jade's beauty, she could handle herself in a fight.

Hannah realized she was staring. Rattled at how sideways her life had gone, she led the way into the house and stepped into the kitchen. She gestured to Riley in the corner. "My sister, Riley."

"Hey, Riley, nice to meet you. I'm Jade. Savage asked me to look out for you guys. You doin' okay?"

Riley nodded. "Werewolves are after Hannah. Did you go to Hogwarts with Savage? He said it's all a big secret, but he trusts us to know. So, you know . . . you can tell us things."

Jade's smile grew wider still. "Well, if Sav trusts you, that says a lot. And yes, I was raised and trained at the Academy of Affinities as well. My adoptive father, Reign, runs it and I teach there."

Before Riley started talking about enrollment, Hannah shifted the focus to the wolf curled up in front of the fireplace. "By what Savage said, I think Myra should've been awake by now. Are you a doctor?"

"Of sorts." In a bulky cable-knit sweater and jeans, Jade didn't look like a doctor. She looked like a model in a sexy Harlequin commercial for curling up with a good book on a cold afternoon.

Jade rubbed her palms together and knelt beside Myra's sleeping wolf form. After a moment, she started singing an enchanting song in a language Hannah had never heard before. Something about the perfection of the melody eased her anxiety and made her limbs feel heavy.

Wrapping herself in the soothing effect, she returned her attention to the counter. The coffee finished percolating, and she needed a cup or two to get her mind working. She busied herself setting out the mugs and cream, milk, and sugar.

When Jade finished examining Myra and straightened, her easy smile wasn't so easy anymore. "Where's Savage?"

Hannah focused on pouring two mugs with her left hand and not spill it on the counter. "He was injured and wet all night. He's resting now, with a high fever. Do you need to wake him?"

Jade shook her head. "In a moment. He pushes himself too hard. Let him rest. There's nothing he can do anyway."

"That doesn't sound good. What's going on?"

Jade held up one finger and dialed up a contact on her phone. "Hey, Bree, I need you here with your kit . . . Some kind of poison . . . Cowboy's mother." Jade frowned. "Yeah, I hear you, but I need you to look past that . . . 'Kay, thanks. See you in a few."

A few? Were Waylon's family reinforcements all able to Flash wherever they liked at will? "Myra's poisoned?"

Jade nodded. "I believe so, yes."

"Will she live?"

Jade shrugged. "If anyone can track the poison and find a treatment, it's Bree."

"Waylon should be here."

Jade accepted a mug of coffee and sipped it black. "He and my brother are at a big Were summit in Africa. There are no interruptions and no access to them until tomorrow. Until then, we'll have to handle things ourselves."

A Were summit in Africa? "I've wondered for years who Waylon was now, and what his life was like. It sounds like he's done well for himself."

Jade smiled. "Cowboy is a happy, respected, and skilled member of the Were community, a loyal soldier, and brother to many of us. He's also a newly mated husband and looking forward to building a family of his own."

Hannah poured the milk, studying the surface of her coffee until it turned the perfect mocha brown. "I'm glad. Really glad. When Savage was here last time, I didn't know Waylon sent him. I've never known what happened to him."

"Savage was here before?"

She nodded. "When my father passed, three years ago, I left a message at the only number I had for Waylon. A few days after the funeral, Savage arrived to help on the farm. I didn't put the two things together until this morning. He just knocked on my door, said he was passing through, and needed the work. It was hard for him to find work unable to speak. He told me his name was Steve."

Jade straightened, her eyes glinting with amusement. "Steve? And you bought that?"

Hannah laughed too, finally able to see the humor in that. "I was in a weird place. My daddy was the beating heart of this ranch and after he passed, I wasn't sure I could make a run of it without him. I knew Waylon would want to know."

"They were close, Cowboy and your father?"

She nodded. "He worked here every summer as a part-time hand. Daddy always said Waylon was strong as a bull with the temperament of a playful calf."

"Nothing has changed there."

Hannah set down her coffee, her hand aching. "Anyway, when Daddy died, it was smack in the middle of harvest, and everyone for miles was busy in their own fields. I needed help and Savage rescued me. I just didn't realize it was all a lie."

She tapped a few more pain tablets onto the counter and was about to take them when Jade touched her hand.

"In our world, to survive, we hide things. To keep things simple for innocents, we hide things. Try not to take that too personally. Savage is a hard man to get a read on, but he's here because he wants to be. He asked me to help, so here I am. We're family, and you saved Cowboy's life, so you are family by extension."

Hannah didn't know what to think about that. "I don't even know why I need help. Why did the wolves kill Jessop and Jed? Why is Myra poisoned? Why try to kill me?"

Jade shook her head. "That's what we need to find out. Until then, Cowboy's mother isn't the only one who's been assaulted. Let me help you with this."

Jade peeled back the wrap on Hannah's wrist and removed Savage's splint. When she began to sing again, the contact of skin-to-skin tingled, soothing Hannah's ache immediately. Two minutes later, Jade stepped away.

Her arm was healed, and the sensation of serenity held strong. What did a doctor "of sorts" mean?

"What language is that song?" Riley asked, her smile bigger than any she'd worn since coming to the farm almost three years ago. "'Cause I've never heard anything like it."

Jade flipped her long, red hair behind her shoulder and smiled. "It's an ancient Elvish ballad. Singing enhances my gift of magical Bard healing."

"Ohmygod, that's so cool." Riley rushed over and stared at my wrist. "Is it really fixed, Hannah? You're not shitting me, right. She did just magically heal your wrist, right?"

Jade winked, and pressed a straight finger to her lips. "You said you get to know things and can keep a secret, right?"

Another knock interrupted Hannah's jumbled thoughts. She glanced toward the front hall, not sure she could take much more. Chief barked and raced to greet their next guest.

Jade patted her shoulder and winked. "I'll get that. You take a sec for yourself." A moment later, Jade returned with a shorter, athletic woman with gunmetal gray eyes and dark brown hair. "Riley and Hannah, this is Bree."

While Jade's smile was warm and genuine, Bree seemed to size her up.

"Bree is Waylon's mate, and a talented biochemist." Jade pointed to an empty spot on the counter for her to put her equipment. "Let's see what can be done for Cowboy's mother, shall we?"

"I still think we should let her rot," Bree said, her scowl as harsh as her words. "We should pull out and let the members of the pack kill each other off. It's all they're good at. Cowboy washed his hands of them long ago."

Jade didn't seem fazed by Bree's rant. "If Cowboy ever changes his mind, it will be easier for him to settle things with his mother if she isn't dead."

Bree set a large case on the counter and unclicked the locks. When she flipped back the lid, she exposed a fancy microscope. "Where's Sav?"

"Down and out," Jade said, setting a black duffle on the floor beside Bree. "Hannah, may I go check on him? Maybe I can get him back on his feet so he can join the fun."

If there existed people who turned into wolves, and women who healed broken wrists, what other wild and unexplainable things did Savage's world hold? Hannah pointed down the back hall toward the bedroom. "He's in the master. Last door on your right."

CHAPTER SEVEN

*T*he next time I woke, it was to the gentle brush and tingle of fingers touching my forehead. Normally, I would've stiffened, raised my defenses, and readied for battle, but I recognized the subtle charge of Jade's magic and the scent of bergamot her skin gave off during healing. I forced my heavy-lidded eyes open and spoke directly into her mind. *Hey, Blaze.*

"Hey, Blaze?" She popped a health-tab into my mouth and tipped a glass to my lips while I swallowed. "You don't write. You don't call. All I get are dumbass excuses from Kobi and Reign about you taking on every entry-level mission coming across the board. Then, I find you burning up and bleeding in a human woman's bed? What's a girl to think?"

Maybe I stayed away too long.

"Maybe?" She leaned forward, the crease between her eyes no longer hidden by the fall of hair. "We all adjusted to life's meaning without the Scourge, Sav. You're the only one who bugged out and never came home."

I deserved that. Honestly, I missed living in Jade's mansion and seeing her every day. Missed the loud dinners with too many nosy opinions. Missed hitting the mats each morning with my fellow warriors to keep sharp and honed.

I missed my family.

With a scowl firmly locked in place, she pulled at the edge of the sheets. "What are we dealing with here because aside from fatigue and a flu, I also sense an infection?"

I held firm on the Egyptian thread count. *Just a chill, a wolf scratch, and a stab wound. I'm good. I called you here for Hannah's safety, and to keep her away from Cowboy's mother.*

Jade waited, brow raised, her emerald eyes so much like Castian's. "Humor me. It's been months since I've seen you and I'm feeling motherly since I had the twins."

That was all the protest I had. I released the death grip on the sheets and let her have her way. Normally, I patched myself up and kept going. A Talon warrior Timex—I took a shit kicking and kept on ticking.

Except, sometimes, I liked a little of Jade's TLC.

She was the only woman, other than Hannah, who touched me with love. Not in a sexual way, but with warmth. Long before we found out we were cousins, before we fought together for more than a decade, before she knew me well, she cared. That meant a lot.

Jade scowled at the blood, both wet and scabbed, covering my side. Drawing an assessing touch across the bite and the stab wound from earlier, she sighed. "This hasn't been an easy twenty-four hours, has it?"

I chuckled. *When is it ever?*

Jade's hands warmed my skin. She released her healing powers, and I closed my eyes and rode the wave of calm and tingly. "Castian told me he returned your powers to you. You could heal this yourself."

Zo said the same thing. I haven't unlocked them. Not sure I want to.

"Because of the woman?"

Partly. She likes simple. Cattle. Ranch. Family. But more so, it's about me.

She continued the healing, and the tissue on my hip knit back together. "You are who life made you. I get it."

I knew she would.

"What about your voice? That might be one thing you want to reclaim."

What's wrong with who I am?

She finished with the touch healing and laid a hand over mine. "Not one thing, but I know how limiting it can be for you. It's a barrier most people don't understand."

Or don't care to.

Jade expression gave no indication of what she thought about that either way. "You'd likely need physical therapy and healing for your vocal cords. I'm here for you if you ever decide to try."

I focused on the wallpaper covering the far wall. Jade never ceased to wheedle her way behind my lines of defense. The only thing that made it tolerable was that she did that with everyone and she would never betray any of us.

I'm sorry I haven't met your babies. I've been . . . Busy wasn't the right word. Neither was lost.

"Searching?" Jade said, her knowing gaze so damned disarming. She cupped my jaw and made me look at her. "You'll find whatever it is. I have no doubt. Just promise that in the meantime, you won't forget where you belong."

I promise.

She leaned forward and kissed my cheek. "Good, because I love you and miss you. Come home."

Movement brought my attention to Hannah standing at the door, my jeans folded in her hands and her mouth hanging open. She stared at me lying naked on the bed, and the intensity of her gaze had my body waking with all kinds of big ideas. I pulled the sheet over my hips before I embarrassed myself in front of Jade.

"Feeling better, I see," Hannah said.

Thanks to the TLC from my two favorite females.

Jade blinked, likely surprised at the declaration, but I didn't care. Being the aloof, broody male was tough work, and I was tired. From now on, I'd say it loud and proud—these were my girls. My cousin. My mate.

It sounded autocratic to call Hannah my mate—and maybe I lived with the Weres too long—but she was mine. I needed to convince her to give me a second chance.

Hannah's jaw flexed as she flung the jeans at the bed and turned on her heel. Her ass swayed as she took her exit and I loved the show of swagger. Man, she fired me up.

"Uh-oh, you better get dressed and go after her," Jade said, barely holding back a smile.

Why? Where the hell is she going?

Jade laughed, handing me my jeans and boxers. "Here you are, naked, with me kissing you and telling you I love you. I think she got the wrong idea. My guess is, you've got some explaining to do."

You think she thinks . . . you and me?

Jade's smile grew wider. "I do. And if it holds any weight, I like her. She's got spunk."

I pulled my bottoms on, the lumpy socks off, and grabbed my weapons. The shirt I had on earlier was on the dresser and I grabbed it on the fly. I jogged out to the living room, the health-tab Jade gave me working wonders to return my strength and vitality.

Bree straightened from her microscope as I passed the kitchen. I hadn't known she was there but didn't have time to find out why. *Where'd Hannah go?*

"Stormed out the door muttering something about Steve being an asshole. Who's Steve?"

I stomped my feet into my boots and tore out into the blinding glare of the winter wonderland. It wasn't hard to find her. Hannah's tracks dragged through the pristine, three-foot drifts and led me straight to the barn.

I found her in fine form. With a pitchfork in her hands, she tossed straw into the pens like a whirling dervish. I kept to a safe distance. I might be brave enough to face Scourge Raiders and evil sorcerers, but a furious Hannah armed with a pronged weapon was a danger to be respected.

I signed, but she refused to look. Banging my rings on the metal rail of the cow pen did nothing but annoy the cattle. Instead of getting up in her grill, which was my go-to instinct, I took another tack. I grabbed a shovel and started cleaning pens while I waited—not so patiently.

Huh, look at me rocking the long game.

It didn't matter how many stalls I mucked or how many bags of feed I carried, I wasn't going anywhere. If I needed to start back at square one to build and earn her trust, I'd do it by working alongside her, the same way I did three years ago, when we first fell for each other.

"Just go. I don't need you here," she said, hosing down the long water trough that ran the length of the barn wall.

No, you don't want *me here. Not the same thing.*

"You should be in bed, not sweating in a barn."

I'm good . . . all fixed up.

She glared, holding her arm up and pivoting her wrist. "Just what kind of doctor knits broken bones given ten minutes and a song?"

A gifted one?

She rolled her eyes. "I get that the reality of things aren't what most people think. I learned that the day my boy-next-door crush collapsed at my feet and turned into a wolf."

Well, that was new intel I could have done without. Picturing her sitting on a fence rail, gazing at Cowboy, shirt off, glistening in the summer sun, was a hit to my ego, but that wasn't her point.

Seeing him shift opened you up to our world but it's far more complicated than that.

"I don't want complicated."

I know. And I'm sorry.

"Maybe, but what pisses me off is that you pretend things will be different this time."

It will. You, me, and Riley. I'll give it up and give you simple. I swear I'll make it work. I'm all-in.

"But I'm not! The more I learn about your world, the more certain I am that Riley and I have no place in it. It was bad enough when you were a military guy, and I expected you to pick up and leave anytime you were called to serve. Now, I'm dealing with magic and Fae and who knows what else. I'm a cattle rancher from Oklahoma."

I fisted my shaking hands, unable to sign. My greatest fear was that life at Haven would be too much for her. That, no matter what went down, she'd never give us a fair chance.

I love you, doc.

She pitched another pile of straw and frowned. "You love me. I love you. It's irrelevant. You left because I don't belong in your life and you were *right*. That's why, when this is wolf stuff is over, I want you to go and leave us be."

Bullshit. You want me gone because I hurt you and you're afraid to trust me. You want to punish me, but you're punishing us both. Me coming from the Realm of the Fair is moot. I'll prove that to you. We'll ranch. I'll make you forget all about my other life. I'll live this life, and we'll be together.

"Maybe that's not what I want."

I pushed the pile of manure I gathered down the alley. By the time I made my way back, Hannah looked like she'd cooled down a bit. *I can read you, doc. I have a lot to make up for, I get that, but you love me, and I love you.*

"And what about Jade? She loves you too. I'm not a jealous person, but hello? She's gorgeous, confident, a magical healer, and—"

Happily married with newborn twins. I smiled as her mind stumbled on that. *I was honest. Jade is gifted, and she's one of my two favorite women, but it's not like that with her. Never has been.*

"I saw the two of you together. She seemed awfully familiar with you lying there naked."

I leaned the shovel against the paint-chipped wall and closed the distance. *Jade has patched me up a hundred times over the last decade. Prudish modesty stopped being an issue years ago. She loves me, but not romantically.*

Gods, I hated to see Hannah struggle. This was good though. She was listening, and I would make her understand.

"When you said your world was different than mine, I thought you meant in morality, or economy, or something. I missed the mark on that completely. It's hard catching up."

It's a lot, I know. My whole life, I was focused on finding and destroying my brother. When the shit hit a few months ago, I found out Jade's biological father and mine are brothers—she's my cousin. I also have four half-sisters I didn't know about. The only one worth knowing, Zophia, just married my best friend, Kobi, and another male, Aust. It's been a mind-fuck all around.

I had pictures on my phone that Zo sent of the wedding. I patted my pocket but realized my phone was in the house. I'd show Hannah the pictures when we got back inside. Maybe seeing how normal and happy they were might help.

"Jade's your cousin?"

She is.

"And you're okay with me asking her to verify all this?"

Ouch. Of course. No lies. No secrets. You're down the rabbit hole now, doc. There has never been anything between Jade and me except friendship and respect.

"What about Bree? She seems to hate me for no reason."

Bree is Cowboy's mate—a coyote. Weres are wildly territorial and protective of what's theirs. Bree probably doesn't like that Cowboy holds you in such warm regard.

"She's jealous of *me*? Seriously? She can turn into a coyote, is married to Waylon, and is jealous of me?"

Why do you sound so surprised? You're strong, capable, beautiful and independent. You share a past and a connection to a life with him that she'll never truly understand. To her base animal, that's threatening. Hell, I find it hard and I've got a healthy ego.

"Don't be stupid." Kicking the shutoff valve with her rubber boot, she continued with the hose as the trough filled with clean water. The cattle jostled forward to drink. "I'm no catch. Absence made your brain go soft. I've got two-hundred-and-sixty-eight head and no idea how to feed them through winter. I'm behind at the bank and my neighbors, who always helped me in the past, are dead or trying to kill me. If I meant anything to Waylon, he'd be here helping me sort his family bullcrap out."

Hannah cut off the water and hung up the hose. She bolted off toward the tack room, and I followed. I sensed her emotional break-down barreling down on her earlier this morning. I didn't blame her.

The past two days had kicked the snot out of all of them.

Grabbing a roll of shop towels off the shelf, I ripped a square free and got dabbing. Hannah knocked me stupid. It didn't matter if she was made up to go out for a night or waking up with her hair wild, or pink and puffy with tears. She blew me away every time I laid eyes on her.

Holding her tight to my chest, I nuzzled the soft hollow of her neck and wished I could whisper comforting words into her ear. I could pay off her debts, but she would never accept. I could take her away, but this farm was her past, present, and future. I had already promised to stay and help her get the ranch back in the black, but she didn't believe me.

I had never felt less like a warrior in my life.

I pushed the collar of her jacket out of the way and pressed my lips to her throat. In the chill of the barn, her skin was balmy warm. I nipped and kissed, smiling against her flesh as she tipped her head back and gave me access.

That's right. Urging her on, I triggered her body's natural pull. That, at least, was one thing that hadn't changed in three years. The connection we shared, the insatiable pull that drew us together, remained as strong now as ever.

I didn't know where we were headed, but Hannah was my home. Wherever she was—

Knocked to the side, I grabbed Hannah and widened my stance to keep from toppling. The earth below us shook. The explosion that rocked the ground sounded like a bomb had gone off in the not too distant distance. *Fuck.*

Wrapping my arms around her, I Flashed out beside the drive shed. The house was a fireball, black smoke vomiting in such volume that the entire front yard was engulfed. My skin crawled with some-thing colder than the chill of the air. Icicles of fear dripped into my chest and started freezing in my veins.

"Riley!" Hannah screamed. I caught her jacket before she got away.

"Let go of me," she spat, fists flying. I evaded the hits, determined to keep her safe. "Riley and your friends are in there. Chief and Myra."

And it wouldn't do any of them any good for Hannah to join them. A vortex of flame rose from the front lawn and drew the thick blanket of smoke into the air.

Hope flared in my hammering heart. That funnel wasn't from the house fire. That blazing shaft of smoke and flame was being commanded.

As the air cleared, I spotted Jade and Bree in the snow. They shielded Riley and fought off five attackers—three of them as wolves. Rage hemorrhaged from every pore.

Hide in the shed, I signed. *I'll get her for you.* I threw myself into a dead run across the yard.

Blaze was one hell of a fighter on offense, but defense got sticky when protecting innocents. Bree hadn't had our training. The coyote girl could fend off humans, and drunken assholes at the Hearthstone, but that was about it. Against male wolves, she was out of her depths.

I targeted her for the save and went in hard.

Five hostile males fought to wrestle the women across the front lawn of the farmhouse. Their meaty hands hung empty of weapons, which was good and no surprise. Weres thought brute strength was all they needed in a fight.

Yeah, well, it wouldn't do them much good against two Glock 40s, fuck-you-very-much. My boots made no sound, my breath coming out in sharp, white puffs. The exertion of racing through knee-deep snow had my sinuses stinging with the icy cold.

As I approached, the wind changed.

Bree lifted her chin and let off a low growl. "Four more coming in," she yelled, kicking a guy in the sac before being flung to the snow.

Four more. I had no idea if they were in wolf or human form, but nine was not a lucky number. I needed to even the odds before they arrived. Flashing forward, I grabbed Riley and Flashed her inside the drive shed.

I didn't stay more than a heartbeat. Releasing her, I pointed to Hannah and Flashed back to the fight.

A wolf howled, rolling in the snow, his pelt on fire. *And that, ladies and gentlemen is how Blaze became Jade's nom de guerre.* The female was a powerful fighter, but she wasn't invincible, and I didn't want her hurt.

Arms raised and sparks flying, she fought and held them back far enough I could get off a couple of shots.

Two fell like rocks.

I took out another, and the world erupted in shouts and growls. Nine was now six—unless more joined the fun.

I evaded a lunging wolf, rolling in the snow and rising back to my boots in one fluid movement. I aimed and shot at any aggressor that moved on us. I wanted the girls safe. I wanted Hannah out of this. She was right. This wasn't her world. She was defenseless against this kind of violence.

A three-inch branch to my forehead had me down and reeling. I lost the use of my legs for a moment as the cracking pain knocked me for a loop. When the Were attacked, I dove right, then rolled left, narrowly escaping the follow-up blows.

Hannah screamed back at the shed, and I cursed.

Rolling to my belly, I watched two men take off. Instinct more than conviction brought my guns back into play. Two shots took one down and left the other rolling to his knees still moving. The branch to my head had done damage. My feet felt sloppy and inefficient under my legs as I ran to help.

Thirty yards from the outbuilding, a massive gray wolf circled from the side, maw wide and teeth exposed. It gripped my shoulder and took me to the ground. The battle of leather against canines went to the wolf.

Pierced flesh burned hot as snow covered my face and neck. Fury fired in my gut and overwrote every other thought. I screamed inside as the beast strengthened its hold and shook. With my free hand, I got my gun up and pumped off four rounds against the fur pelt.

The wolf was possessed. It didn't release, and two others were closing in fast. A bolt of fire hit, and the wolf howled like a demon. Heat blasted my arm, but I took my freedom and pulled back before Jade's fireball torched my skin.

Normally, I thrived on the chaos of battle, but not today. Not like this. Staggering to my feet, I fought to close the gap between Hannah and me.

Long streams of flames erupted on both sides of me, clearing my path like a fiery airport runway. Hannah saw me coming and ran back inside the shed. I lost track of one of the wolves gunning down on her and scanned the scene.

I pushed hard, breath sawing in my lungs, blood blinding me as I ran. What was worth all this death? Pack politics? Nothing was worth Hannah's life.

I rounded the doorframe of the massive shed and found them. Hannah stood before her sister, swinging a scythe like a maniac. The Were before them was searching for his opening.

Not gonna find one, *bitch!*

I set my guns on the fender of the tractor and lifted an arm to catch Hannah's attention. *Drop on three*, I signed.

She nodded, her eye's flashing between the wolf and me for the count.

One. Two. Three.

Reclaiming both guns, I targeted the Were in the back of the head and heart. Firing both in unison, the beast had no chance. The breathy gasp of death satisfied something inside me that I never looked too closely at.

I listed to the side and used my good shoulder against the tractor tire to bounce back onto my path to the girls.

"Savage," Hannah cried, running to catch me as my knee buckled and I went down to the dirt floor. She dropped the scythe and knelt at my hip. "What can I do? Are you okay?"

Peachy, I thought. I was about to respond when a russet wolf trampled me, grabbed Hannah by her jacket, and threw her back. The impact knocked my guns from my blood-slick hands, and punctured something in my chest.

Lung, I guessed.

I rolled to the side and choked for breath, the long wooden handle of the scythe meeting my hands as if willed there by Castian himself. I took the win and swung.

My first swipe sliced the beast's hind leg. The second vivisected him. Guts spilled onto the ground and Riley gagged somewhere behind me. Dizzy and gasping, I hit the cold ground of the shed and blinked up at the beamed roof.

Look through the cracks, I signed. *What's happening.*

Hannah's tears fell like a summer downpour, hot on my face. I struggled with my hands, losing motor control. *Doc. The girls. Tell me.*

My sketchy vision blurred. Fading consciousness flipped me the bird. Between blood loss and asphyxiation, I was tapping out. A cold spot clenched my heart. It didn't matter how big a badass you were. Eventually, the Reaper found you.

CHAPTER EIGHT

*H*annah watched Savage lose consciousness, and a panicky fear screamed in her ears. If he couldn't help them, what chance did they have? Savage fought with violent intensity. He killed with unchecked brutality. Had he given his life to ensure they survived? Honoring his wishes, she raced to the shed wall and peered through a crack between weathered boards.

The last man standing was Jonas Brooke.

Jonas owned the Feed and Seed out on the highway. Given his small stature and meek personality, she'd never realized he was part of Jessop's pack. Staring at the carnage on her front lawn, he seemed stunned. Dead wolves. Wounded and singed men.

He turned, arms up to the sky like he was a televangelist Werewolf preacher. "It didn't have to be this way, Hannah. If you'd been honest about Myra seeking you out and given us the ring, this could have been avoided."

The ring? What ring?

"Hannah?" Riley yelled. "Hannah!"

Hannah spun in time to see Levi Dunn grab her sister and vanish. She ran at the blank space, her heart thundering like she'd run a four-minute mile.

Sirens of emergency vehicles wailed in the distance.

"Jessop may have tolerated you knowing about us," Jonas yelled from outside. "He can't protect you anymore. There's nowhere for you to hide. We've got your sister. The only way you get her and your friends back is to give us the ring. We expect to hear from you soon."

She held her breath as Jonas signaled to two men and they disappeared with Riley, Jade, and Bree. Could everyone in Savage's world do that?

Jonas's words rang in her head. Jessop had known she knew all along? Had he known she saved Waylon?

Savage choked and she rushed over to roll him onto his side. *What's happeinging.*

She knelt over him, her entire body numb. "They're gone."

Are we accounted for?

Hannah shook her head. "Jonas and his men took Riley, Jade, and Bree to trade for a ring? I don't know what that means but that's what he said."

Jessop's Alpha ring. The wearer rules the pack.

"Mercy, you're losing a lot of blood. I need to get you to a hospital."

Savage frowned and shook his head. *No time.* He fumbled a bloody hand toward his pocket and winced.

"What do you need?"

Phone.

She searched both his pockets and both of hers. "No phone. What now?"

Resignation clouded his gaze, and he closed his eyes.

Her heart sank. "Don't you dare give up on me, Savage. You can't come back after three years to tell me you love me and then die. That's not fair. You said you wouldn't leave."

He opened heavy-lidded eyes and cracked a crooked smile. *I wasn't dying. I was thinking.*

She swallowed. "Oh. Sorry. What did you come up with? Anything good?"

Unlock my god powers.

She had no idea what that meant, but didn't care. "Then unlock them."

It'll change me. Complicate things.

So? What good did it do either of them if he refused to change and died? "Go on. Do it before you pass out again."

Nothing happened, and her heart broke. Didn't he know his life was worth anything and everything that came at them? She swallowed, her throat thick and tight. "Whatever it takes, you do it. Survive, dammit. You promised you'd never leave me again. Was that another lie? You swore to me, Savage."

He closed his eyes again, and she wasn't sure if he was doing something or passing out. Tears dripped off her cheeks onto his face. "If you die now, the loss of our future is on you. Are you a quitter?"

His hands shifted. *Shhh. Can't concentrate.*

"Oh," she whispered. "Sorry."

Biting her bottom lip, she watched his eyelids flicker. His body stiffened straight as a board and Hannah felt the energy in the frigid air crackle around her. She backed up a few inches to give him space.

What did unlocking god powers mean?

She'd seen what Jade could do. His cousin shot fire from her hands, and could fight off four wolves and Were men at a time. Given what Savage could already do without powers, she imagined he'd become a truly lethal one-man army.

That scared her for about two seconds. Savage might be King of Broody, but he had a code of honor that placed him right up with military superheroes in her mind.

A tremor shook his body, and she gripped his hand in hers. "I'm here, tough guy. I'm right here with you."

His eyes flipped open, the blank orbs in his skull glowing silver. Her breathing hitched, her tears blurring her vision. She choked. If he did this for her and it was the wrong decision for him . . . "I'm so sorry."

Alone and helpless, all she could do was hold his hand and ramble on about things she thought, felt, and should have told him before he was dying.

"I forgive you." She wiped her face on the sleeve of her ruined jacket. "You sacrificed what we were building for the good of others—I get that—but you made one mistake. You should've told me. I would've understood. I would've waited. You need to make it up to me."

Emergency vehicles crunched through the snow outside. Harsh male voices started shouting off commands. Savage's body sagged to the ground, and the color in his eyes morphed to the same brilliant emerald green as Jade's.

"Hey there," she said, swiping at her eyes. "Gaw, I'm such a mess." He lifted his hand to her cheek and slid to the back of her neck. His lips were cold, and she had to wipe the tears and snot off him when she pulled back. She rubbed his stubbled cheeks with her palms, her heart racing. "Are you okay, now? Is it over?"

A lot is bombarding me, but I'll live. Hannah helped him sit up and steadied him when he lilted. *Can I get a recap? My brain is fried. Oh, and my guns.*

Hannah stepped away, watching his gentle sway while she grabbed his weapons. "Jonas took Jade, Bree, and Riley. He said he'd exchange them for Jessop's ring. You said it was an Alpha thing, to take over the pack? I don't know where they took them, but I do know how to track them down."

She muscled Savage to his feet. Not much was left of her yard beyond the fire trucks, sheriff cars, and the ambulance parked harum-scarum in every direction. The vehicles blocked the path from her truck, parked in the drive shed, to the lane.

No emergency call necessary. Black smoke billowed up from what once was her family home. The plume darkened the gray, wintery sky with the destruction of the only life she'd ever known or wanted. She searched the crowds, hoping to catch sight of Chief checking out the action. Had he gotten out of the house before the explosion?

She couldn't think about that. "Blink us to town."

Savage shook his head. *Too scrambled.*

"We need to get out of—Tandy!" She waved her part-time farmhand through the chaos of emergency workers and met him with a one-armed hug. "Where's your truck, cowboy?"

"I couldn't get any closer than the willow that overhangs the lane."

"Perfect. Give me your keys." She held out her hand and, bless his heart, he never even asked why. "Check the livestock and get everyone settled and bedded down. I need to run to town. If I'm not back by the time you're ready to leave, take my truck from the shed, and we'll switch back later."

"Hannah," Billy Upton said, jogging over from a conversation with the fire chief. "You can't go anywhere. I need to take your statement. Where's your sister? Did this man have anything to do with the fire?"

Hannah turned as Billy's partner, Luke, and two of the local police department flanked Savage. The four of them looked like they were corralling a wild bull and she didn't miss their hands perched on their sidearms.

Savage, however, looked like he might collapse on the lawn at any moment. Covered in blood, his jacket ripped, his legs barely holding him upright, he wasn't the picture of violent intent he usually projected.

"He had nothing to do with this. He saved my life."

"Then let's have you both checked out. You can start from the beginning and tell us what happened."

She stared at her house smoldering in the snow and fought not to cry. "I honestly don't know what happened, Billy. The two of us were in the barn. We heard the explosion and came running."

"He was with you?"

"Yes, Billy. He worked for me a few years back as a hand and was checking in. That's all I know right now, but I gotta get to town."

"Hannah, anything you need from town can wait till tomorrow, I'm sure. What's your name, buddy," he said directly to Savage. "You sure don't look like you're from around here."

She shook her head, both to answer Billy, and as a warning to Savage who, although he didn't look like it at that moment, could single-handedly take out the Woodsboro Creek fire, police, and sheriff's departments all at once. "Sorry, Billy, it really can't wait. I gotta go get Riley."

Billy tilted his head, his face screwed up with either the heat of the fire or the glare off the snow. "You seem squirrelly. Everything all right, Hannah?"

"No, *Billy*," she snapped. "Everything is *not* all right. My house blew up. Things are as far from all right as they get." She turned and stormed off, thankful Savage's heavy foot-falls seemed to strengthen with each step.

"All right, Miss Hannah," Luke said, chasing them down, obviously setting in to be the voice of reason. "How 'bout you introduce us to your friend, so we can add his name to our report. Then, we'll check things out while you're gone."

Hannah rolled her eyes and wondered if anyone's head actually did explode? *Lord save me from well-meaning men.* "You mean check *him* out, not *things*, don't you Luke?"

Luke looked from her to Savage, and back. "I know you said he was a friend and all, but—I mean, Billy counted five or six dead wolves, which makes no sense. We're trying to get to the bottom of what happened. There's a lot of blood in the snow and footprints and evidence of one hell of a commotion, and he's a stranger covered in blood. By the way he's dressed, and those tattoos—"

"You're *not* going to say something offensively stupid now, are you, Luke? This is still America, right? Freedom to express oneself. Innocent until proven guilty. Any of that sounding familiar?"

Luke frowned. "Well, I know you're upset, Hannah, but there's no need to be hostile. We don't get many houses blowin' up, and this guy—"

"Had nothing to do with it. Take my word for it, Luke, don't judge this book by its cover. You'll be wrong."

The fire chief whistled from around the side of the house and Hannah gave him a wave of acknowledgment. "Looks like they need you. Please figure out what happened. Once I get Riley, we'll stop by the station and go over everything we know with you then."

The distraction seemed to break whatever spell of small-minded stupidity Luke suffered from. He relaxed and took a step back. "Yeah, okay. You're vouching for him, though, and if we need to find him, we're coming to you."

Hannah nodded. "Good enough."

Glad to be out from under the microscope, she sorted the keys as they jogged to Tandy's truck and hopped in the driver's side. "Sorry about that. Honestly, I can't believe you didn't break someone's neck."

If it didn't slow us down more than those dumbass questions, I would have.

CHAPTER NINE

I collapsed against the seat and Hannah made quick work of turning Tandy's truck around and getting us the hell gone. The snow was stupid deep on the lane, but soon enough, we fishtailed onto the newly plowed country road. The engine of the beat-up old Ford four-by-four choked and growled as the road conditions improved, and Hannah revved things up.

"No phones, so I guess we're on our own?"

For the moment. The bastards who took the girls would fucking rue the day. This was my fault. I involved Jade, and she brought in Bree. If anything happened to either of them, it was on my head, and Cowboy would never forgive me. If anything happened to Riley, Hannah would never forgive me.

Which was fair, because I wouldn't forgive myself.

As the landscape flew by, I tried to focus. Unlocking my powers scrambled my brain at a time when I needed to think. Head reeling and body aching, my ears still buzzed under the onslaught of Fae energy. It bombarded. It invaded. It spread through my muscles and cells, changing me.

I didn't want this. Hannah wanted normal. I wanted to be what she needed. What would being a demi-god do to us?

I love you, I signed, even though her eyes were locked on the road ahead. I'd buried how much until I saw her on the ground with that first Were holding a gun to her head. Bile roared up my throat just thinking of it. Never again.

I'd make sure of it.

She blew through the flashing caution light at the intersection of two country roads and another wave of nausea struck. I tucked my hands under my armpits and tried to still the shaking of my hands. I had to make this work.

Hannah forgave me.

During those dark moments in the drive shed, while my head threatened to explode and my cells were overheating, the tether that kept me anchored in place was her hold on my hand, and her voice in my ear.

I forgive you. Three little words that gave me the strength to endure. Soon, I'd coax her into saying those other three little words I want to hear.

Not as an admission, but as a declaration.

My throat tightened, trying to swallow past something that wasn't there. What kind of bastard was I that I was grateful Hannah sat safely beside me and when the others were in the clutches of angry wolves?

Was that fucked up, or what? This whole thing was.

Staring out the side window, I studied the land as it stretched off for miles and miles. Fields bordered the thickly forested land shared by Cowboy's family and the families of his pack. The Werewolves lived, worked, and thrived among their unaware human neighbors. They were the family next door. The bartender at the local pub. The lady who played the organ at church.

They were Hannah's friends, and they'd turned on her.

"Why are you growling?"

This pack didn't know a damned thing about loyalty. *Cowboy is one of the greatest men I know. He should've lived happily among his pack, grown up with his parents, and dated girls from high school. Instead, he was tossed like garbage. It pisses me off.*

Hell, Cowboy might have ended up with Hannah if he'd been

allowed to stick around. He was her crush, afterall. Energy built up inside me and burst out in a wave. A telephone pole transformer burst into flames as we passed, throwing sparks into the dull, January sky.

Yeah, time to focus on the now.

How could I find them? Surely these powers must offer some advantage over sleuthing it on the ground for the next hours. I needed to move quickly. I needed to track Were movement. If Zo was still the Fate for Lives in Progress, she could pull the tapestries of that Jonas guy. She wasn't.

She gave up her station when our sisters fucked her over, and she started her new life at Haven. Now she only watched over—bingo.

"Welcome to the Whippoorwill," Hannah said to nobody, pulling the truck into the only empty parking spot in sight. She had no idea where Savage had poofed off to. Then again, it wasn't the first time he left her wondering where he went. His absence didn't change much. She still needed to find out where Riley was. She still needed to find out who was behind it all. And she still needed to convince the wolves she had no idea about any Were ring.

Woodsboro Creek's Were watering hole was the place to do all three. If anyone knew about the attack on Jessop and where Riley and the others were, they'd be inside.

She considered waiting on Savage, but Riley needed her. Besides, it wasn't like anyone would kill her in the middle of a local diner, with a dozen human neighbors enjoying their pie.

The Whippoorwill Café sat on the wheat field outskirts of her sleepy Oklahoma town. On the easternmost end of a strip plaza, it was neighbor to the barbershop/tool sharpening business, Clips & Clippers, and the pool hall, which also doubled as a non-denominational church on Sundays.

Main Street was bustling despite the dumping of snow over the past two days. Lots of movement along the streets and sidewalks. Plenty of witnesses to keep her safe.

Before she caught the handle of the truck door, she drew a deep breath. She could do this. Popping the glovebox, she dug around, searching for a weapon of some sort. A Swiss Army knife was all she found. It would have to do.

Rounding the hood, she wished she had her Colt. Not that she wanted to shoot any of her friends, still, prepared would be better. Despite herself, she wished Savage was there to help her handle this.

But he wasn't. Big surprise. She forgave him, but down deep, where it mattered—she didn't. Her brain understood. Her heart still ached.

As she approached the Whippoorwill, she glanced through the plate-glass windows to see who was inside. The place was perma-packed with brawny males, muscled females, and the human women who flocked there in droves to ogle them.

Yeah, except when they were trying to kill you, that brawny, muscled physique wasn't quite so sexy.

It was terrifying.

Despite her fear for Riley, she had to keep levelheaded. As the bell over the door sounded, she waved to the blonde working behind the long breakfast counter and headed straight into the wolf den.

Striding across the restaurant, she kept her step strong and took note of anyone who looked surprised and, in a couple of cases, alarmed to see her. When she reached the Formica counter, she leaned across and hugged her friend.

"Jayne, hey, I'm sorry about Jessop. I know you were close. How are you?"

She and Jayne had been friends since ninth grade. The two of them had spent endless Friday nights watching Waylon and the others playing football down at the stadium.

With a sigh, Jayne grabbed three plates off the heated rail and paused, staring at the scrape on Hannah's cheek. "Better than you, I expect."

"I assume you know what's going on?"

"It's a small community, hon. I expect I know about as much as everyone else. I'm not sure if you coming here is incredibly brave or unbelievably stupid."

"Stupid? Carter attacked me. Jonas kidnapped Riley. What am I supposed to do, sit at home and wait to be killed? No, wait. I don't have a home. Your friends *blew it up*."

Jayne cast her a cool glare, and Hannah met the scrutiny matching every ounce of regret and determination. For the first time in their lives, they were on opposite sides of a critical line.

It hurt to know where she stood when the chips fell. But at least she knew. They remained in their ocular standoff until a fat trucker by the door broke the spell.

"Hey, JayJay?" he yelled from his four-top. "Any chance you'll bring lunch before my break's over? I gotta get back on the road."

"Keep your pants on, Gerry. You're not going to wither away if you miss a meal." That earned Jayne a few laughs from the other patrons. With the plates balanced up her arms, she hooked a condiments carrier and took Gerry his lunch.

Hannah's head pounded behind her eyes. Who was behind this? Who could she talk to? Normally, she'd go to Jessop and Myra, but they were dead.

"Hey, babe. Been a tough couple of days?" Matt offered her his usual winning smile as he pulled her to his chest. A buff, good-looking, all-American athlete type, he knew darn well the effect of his smile on women. Despite how it annoyed her, she wasn't immune. She'd gone a few rounds with Matt off and on over the years. "I'm glad you're here. Let's go somewhere private and talk."

Her heart revved, adrenaline coursing from her chest out to the trembling tips of her fingers. Hannah pressed her palms flat on his flannel button-down and took a step back. "Private time with you is over, Matt. Public conversations suit me better now, thanks. My question is, who should I talk to?"

Matt cast a dismissive glance and shrugged. "That depends. Did you bring the ring? It was stupid of you and Myra to think you could go up against us and win."

What was with this town? Hannah offered Matt a tight smile. "I didn't go up against anyone. I have no idea what sparked the trouble, or how I suddenly became targeted, but blowing up my house and kidnapping Riley and women from my home crossed a line."

Matt's jaw clenched as he leaned close. "Do you honestly not get what's happening here?"

Hannah gave him a well-duh stare. "I honestly don't. I found Myra in the creek, freezing and unconscious, and took her home to warm her by the fire. Then, suddenly, I'm being thrown from my horse and have a gun to my head. Then Jonas comes today in another wave of crazy, and says he wants a ring—which I neither have nor know anything about. Whatever this is, it's been badly handled, and I'm sick of being in the middle of it."

The heads of people sitting at the nearby tables turned as her voice grew momentum, and she could see by Matt's reaction, he didn't like being told off in public. Too bad.

"Who's acting as Alpha?" she said, loud enough that a whole lot of men bristled. Several of them stood.

Matt frowned. "You think you know about us? What did Myra tell you?"

"Myra didn't tell me anything. You guys drugged her and blew her up. What the hell is wrong with you people?"

Matt grabbed her by the lapels of her coat and lifted her off her feet. "Don't say I didn't warn you."

"Let her go." Blake emerged from the kitchen. She wasn't fooled by his round belly or his Kiss the Cook apron. Blake was as dangerous as the rest of them. "Hannah, there are a lot of innocent friends in here. This is not the place."

"Was my house the place, Blake?" Hannah snapped. "Did you think I was in it? Or Riley? Were *we* supposed to blow up with Myra and end your pathetic little takeover? If I didn't have friends over, would you be toasting our deaths?"

He waved his hands at Jayne and the other server. They hustled over with takeout boxes and got several couples to clear out. The mass exodus left Hannah alone in the company of an angry pack of Weres. "Now, if you can be civil, maybe we can work this out."

"Please, you animals don't know what civility is. Your answer to everything is dumb brute force."

Blake growled, his eyes flipping gold. "You should watch your mouth, farm girl. I'm the only thing between you walking out of here or getting ripped to shreds."

Hannah laughed, her head edging toward total detonation. "You never expected me to live this long. You're certainly not letting me walk out of here. You want the ring. I want Riley and my friends. It's a simple trade."

"You said you didn't have the ring," Matt said.

Weres could smell lies, so she had to be very careful. "No. I said that I had no idea how I became a target, that I knew nothing about the ring or why you'd want to kill Jessop and Myra."

"But now you do know about the ring?"

"Yes, I do." And she did. Savage had told her that the Pack Alpha wore an insignia ring which granted the wearer power over the pack and the right to rule the members. She'd seen that ring on Jessop's right ring-finger her whole life.

She didn't know where it was, but that wasn't what he asked. As long as she could keep him from asking, maybe she could negotiate.

"Okay, Hannah, so tell me. Where is the Alpha's ring?"

Oh, cowpucks.

Between one thought and the next, I found myself standing in the grand living room of my sister's massive home. Shit. I spun on my heel and gave her my back. Not only did I just abandon Hannah in Oklahoma, but the image of Zophia macking with Aust on the couch was now forever emblazoned in my mind's eye.

Sorry. New powers. I said into her mind. *I didn't mean to beam here. My bad.*

Zophia laughed behind him. "It would've been more awkward in another few minutes, so be thankful you're here now. What can I do for you? If your powers brought you here, you must want to speak with me."

I need to locate Jade and Bree. We were ambushed by rogue Weres, and they were taken, along with an innocent girl.

"Taken?" She brushed past me, her pretty blue skirt rippling behind her as she ran. "Were they hurt?"

Not that I know of. Honestly though, if Jade were conscious, they wouldn't be gone. She's got enough juice to get them out. The longer they're missing, the worse my gut twists, thinking things went south.

Zophia led the way into one of the large guest rooms down the hall. Near the window, a loom sat threaded and empty. Along the far wall, rows and rows of tapestries hung in open-ended wood frames.

Mid-stride, she raised her hands, and a gust of wind rustled the tapestries. Obeying her call, two woven accounts of life came flying to the forefront. She locked one into a wooden frame while Aust rushed in beside her to lock the second one down.

"Who is it, *neelan?*" he asked. "Who has been taken?"

She raised her finger to her husband and focused on the tapestries. "They're together and alive, but that doesn't tell us much. We'd learn more from Zinnia's seeing bowl."

Is she still in the wind with Dane?

"Yes, but her bowl was returned and is up with Zora and Zana in the Hall of Destiny."

Those bitches won't tell me shit.

"But lucky for you, I still hold the Fate ability to command the bowl." Zo grabbed Aust's hand and squeezed it. "I'll be right back. Don't worry. I'll explain later."

The two of us materialized Behind the Veil and onto the steps of the Hall of Destiny. As Castian's sanctum in the heavens, few people had access to come and go Behind the Veil. We did, both by privilege of our stations and by the Fae god blood running in our veins.

"Okay, big entrance," Zo said, taking the ascent on a run. She pushed her hands out in front of her, and the doors flew open. The thundering echo of wood on marble had our two half-sisters squealing and ducking for cover. "Hello, sisters. It's family reunion time."

I followed, hard on Zo's heels. The more time I spent with her, the more I liked her. Standing next to two of the other three Fates, I regarded the three of them together. Zana and Zora both shared her dark hair, iridescent skin, and midnight blue eyes, but that's where the similarity ended.

Zophia had courage and morals and loyalty—all characteristics she learned from her mother, Shalana. Sadly, the other girls had their father, Dane, as their role model, and he was a corrupt, selfish asshole.

"Don't worry, girls. We aren't staying." Zophia sat at the center bowl of three—past, present, and future. "Show me Jade and Bree."

After waiting a brief moment, she swiped her fingers through the golden water and started tugging at appearing images. "Okay, got them. And yep, things are going badly. Grab my hand."

I did as she commanded. I might be a Talon warrior and Fae god on my father's side, but Zo was Fae goddess royalty off the charts. Both parents, plus the gifted powers of her dying mother. She was scary powerful.

We materialized into the center of what looked to be an antique car warehouse. Riley was tied up and trussed to a chair. Jade was out cold on the floor. And three Weres were roughing up Bree, trying to strip her and pin her down.

A growl ripped from my throat. I combated every kind of heinous violence against innocents but at the top of my list of vile was a male forcing himself on a female.

And for it to be someone I cared about—*I've got this.*

Rushing forward, I pulled the first one off and twisted his neck so hard he fell to the ground, looking down at his own ass. I stomped the second one's knee sideways and snapped it like a twig. While that one fell, screaming obscenities, I drew my gun and squeezed off two into the skull of number three.

Dropping my aim, I finished number two as well.

Bree was crouched against a wooden crate, her coyote flashing gold in her eyes.

You're safe now, Bree. I got you. I had no idea if she could read my hands in the state she was in. *Zo. She's more animal than woman right now. See if you can reach her with your Dr. Doolittle powers. She probably doesn't want a man near her right now anyway.*

With Bree in good hands, I flashed Riley an *'okay'?* She nodded, and I headed straight to Jade. Aside from one hell of an egg on the back of her head, she seemed otherwise unharmed. After all the fire-balls she'd been throwing around, this might be half crack-to-the-cranium, and half out-of-juice exhaustion. As far as I could tell, she was simply out cold.

I shifted her onto a car cover and went for Riley next. Pulling my dagger from my thigh sheath, I waited for her to realize what I was doing. I needn't have worried. The kid was calm and collected.

I cut her free from her bindings and let her pull the duct tape off her mouth herself. The moment her mouth was back in business, she launched from the chair and against my chest.

"Thank you, thank you, thank you. I knew you'd find us. I knew you'd kick their asses. When they started horndogging Bree, I didn't know what to do. I worried you might not get here in time."

"But he did," Jade said, wincing. She tried to straighten but gave up and laid back down. "Thanks for the save, Sav."

I laid my cheek on the top of Riley's head and closed my eyes. *Okay, you guys get home. I gotta find Hannah.*

"Fuck that," Bree said, spitting blood onto one of the dead wolves curled up on the floor. "We're all-in until this is over. I've been blown up, beat up, and now I'm pissed. You're not sidelining us now, Sav."

"Sidelining? No. I'm going too," Riley said, pulling back. "If Hannah's in trouble, I'm not sitting around not knowing what's going on."

"Me either," Zo chimed in.

Jade pulled herself to her feet and probed the back of her head. "When have I ever missed out on a party?"

I knew better than to argue with four strong females. Pulling Riley tight against my chest, I nodded my defeat. *Okay, Zo, where to next?*

~

"Hannah!" I grabbed Riley's shirt and kept the kid from running to her sister. Materializing into the diner, with Jade, Zo, and Bree flanking me, it became obvious immediately that we arrived in the nick of time. The relief on Hannah's face lit me up, and yeah, I totally felt like the badass my press-kit said I was. Score one to the good guys.

"It's about time you got here," Hannah said, sagging into the hold of the wolf holding her up. "I was spinning my wheels here and losing traction."

"Let her go, Matt," Riley said, pulling at his hold. I handed her off to Jade and gave her the signal to calm the hell down. "You think you're hot shit, but we've got the fricken Fae gods on our side, asshole. Sucks to be you."

Jade chuckled and wrapped an arm around the kid's shoulder. "Look at the dumb expressions. You don't know what you don't know, right?" She gave me a nod, and I felt the truck parked on my chest ease off.

We had this. Still, I worried. *Are you strong enough for a fight, Blaze?* I asked on our gods wavelength.

She winked. *S'all good. Go get the girl.*

I didn't have to be told twice. Beelining it for the frat boy manhandling Hannah, I got my groove on. My muscles burned to strike. Every violent instinct I possessed rushed hot to the forefront. I had no right to be furious about this guy's familiarity with Hannah. It didn't mean I wasn't.

I growled long and low. The aggressive sound rolled from my throat, and I assessed the males who stiffened, drawn by the challenge. The scraping of chair legs against tile floors set the stage for what was building to be an all-out brawl.

Living with the King of Weres and his Beta taught me tons about the etiquette of the species. Growling at a territorial male wolf surrounded by his pack was dumbass stupid, but it got everyone's attention. I wanted him overconfident. It was the only way he'd give up Hannah without a struggle.

My shitkickers thumped hard as I approached the beat-down. Mutt responded exactly as planned. Tossing Hannah at an empty booth, he readied for impact.

A lifetime of training had me *waaaay* overqualified for this dipshit. I ducked the swing, grabbed the guy by the wrist, spun, and had him pinned face down on a bussed table before anyone blinked.

A quick grab to my thigh had a dagger pressed to loverboy's throat. Unless I missed my guess, good ole Matt played cock of the walk because he was on the inner circle and thought he had things all figured out.

"Let him go," the fatso cook thundered out from behind the counter and frowned. "Who the fuck do you people think you are? Do you have any idea the trouble you're in? Boys, cover the exits."

Bree laughed as Weres took position, blocking the doors. "Oh, this is going to be good. Waitress, can the kid and I get some popcorn for the big reveal here in a moment?"

Jade flipped back the cuff of her sweater and fingered the skirl wrapped and tied around her wrist with a leather thong. Each of Bruin's siblings possessed one of his enchanted bear-claw whistles.

"Is that a dog whistle—"

"No, it's a brother whistle." She raised the long, polished claw to her mouth and blew.

Bruin materialized beside his sister, gun drawn and looking homicidal. Cowboy Flashed in beside him a milli-second later.

"Blaze?" Bruin said, taking in the crowd. "What's happened? Where are we?"

Cowboy took three long strides and pulled Bree against his chest. He brushed a gentle finger over the scuff on her cheek, then took in her torn clothes and the bruises coming up on her neck. A deadly warning rumbled from through the diner. "We're in fucking Woodsboro Creek and this is my pack. Will someone please tell me what the fuck happened to my mate?"

Stepping in front of Hannah and her sister, I blocked access to my girls. With this much power on Team Haven, we were good, but I wasn't taking chances. When the two hugged me from behind, I stood tall, feeling indestructible.

The movement caught the attention of Cowboy, and he straightened. "Hannah? What's happened?"

"I'm sorry, Waylon," she said, her voice choked. "Your mate was hurt trying to save my sister and me."

"Save you from what?"

"Your pack killed your family, and I got tangled up in it. They wanted the Alpha ring and think I have it."

There was a momentary flash of pain in the guy's caramel-colored eyes, and then it was gone. "Who? When?"

"Lock us down, Blaze," Bruin said, circling his finger in the air. The instant pressurizing of Jade's magical seal made my ears pop. A couple of chair legs scratched the floor and Bruin shook his head. "For anyone with big ideas, wondering who the fuck just prevented you from leaving, I'm Bruin, your King, and my fucking ring trumps them all, assholes."

The Weres fell silent as Hannah, Jade, and Bree recounted the past few days. I zoned out, content with the arms of two girls clinging tight around my waist. I winked back at Riley, who seemed to be having the time of her life.

Yeah, we were all soaked and filthy from rolling around in the snow and on cold dirt and concrete floors. We'd take care of that soon enough. I planned to take them home, soak with Hannah in a hot bath, and warm her up, both inside and out.

When the ladies were done their recap, Bruin sat on one of the tables and swept his palm through the air. "This is all you, Cowboy. Handle this however you want."

Bree laughed. "Payback time, bitches."

Cowboy kissed the top of Bree's head and stepped away. He paced the room, meeting the confused gazes of younger wolves and the frightened gazes of the older. How many of them were involved in the attack that left Cowboy near death?

"You know," Cowboy said, meandering between the tables, the heels of his boots bumping the tile with each step, "I never thought I'd be back. I came to terms with my pack despising me, and my parents betraying me. My best revenge was living an honorable life, seizing each day, and protecting the innocent—like one amazing person did for me."

He stopped in front of Hannah and the hug he gave her lifted her off her feet and brought a glorious smile to her face. "Thank you, Banana."

She beamed. "By the praise of your friends, it sounds like you did real good."

"Right?" he said, his smile hitting Bruin, Bree, Jade, and then me. "I'm the Beta to the Were King. I'm mated to a beautiful coyote girl who's got way more brains than to fall for a goof like me, and I have the kind of love and family support I'd never get here."

"Damn straight," Jade said.

"And that's the problem." He picked up a bag of chips from below the register and opened them up. Popping one in his mouth, he chewed and shook his head. "I get what my father tried to do here, but he did it through politics and backstabbing. He was ruthless and, in turn, his pack grew to be untrustworthy assholes."

I raised my hands. *They don't know a thing about loyalty.*

Cowboy nodded. "Exactly my point, Sav."

"How many are in the pack now?" Bruin asked, looking around expectantly.

"Forty-six at the last moon run," the blonde waitress, Jayne, answered.

Cowboy wrote forty-six on a menu pad and looked up. "Okay, forty-six, less my family, and how many more?"

I started the tally. *Two in the pasture. Four in the barn. Two in the drive shed that day. How many walked away from the nine that attacked us in the yard?*

"Originally, three," Jade said. "A guy named Jonas and two injured."

And now?

107

"Well, the Jonas guy tried something very ungentlemanly on Bree, and the others backed him up, so that number had to be adjusted."

Cowboy's eyes flipped gold as his wolf ascended. "What is their current status?"

Bree shrugged and offered her mate a sweet smile. "They no longer have names in the living column of the pack roster."

"Good," he said, his pacing trail taking him back on a loop to kiss his bride. "Down to twenty-six. Almost forty-five percent of the pack is dead in two days because you've all been groomed to think you're tough-as-shit top-of-the-heap untouchable. Does anyone else think that's fucked up?"

"It's arrogant," Bree said, "and it's because they live here in a pocket among humans. If they were in the Realm of the Fair, they'd learn humility pretty fucking quick."

"Bullshit," Blake said, his round face getting redder by the moment. "You think I'll believe that this ink-splash hoodlum and those two girls took out seventeen full-grown males from our pack? That would take an army."

I lit up with a shit-eating grin and wished I could tell them that his guys were fermenting under six feet of cow dung. Being mute sucked some days.

Hannah caught my expression and almost laughed. "No army. Just one Talon Enforcer here to check on me, and two very skilled and talented women."

Jade waved away the compliment. "It's all in the raising. Where Cowboy's father was a brute, I was brought up by two fathers. My biological father is Castian, God of gods, and the man who raised me is Maximus Reign. You all might know him as the Reign of Terror? Well, both had gifts to give and lessons to teach."

"Speaking of Reign," Bruin said, looking to Cowboy and waving his phone. "I texted him the sitch. You stay and decide what you want to be done with this pack. I gotta get back to Africa."

Cowboy chuckled. "When's he coming?"

"I mentioned Jade was taken prisoner and roughed up, so . . . uh, now."

As the words left Bruin's mouth, Reign Flashed in, looking murderous. Then Kobi, Sin, and Rue. Then Nash and Samuel. The Whippoorwill filled up with men in leather, and the Weres in the room looked sick.

I chuckled and kissed Hannah's cheek.

The Cavalry is here.

CHAPTER TEN

*H*annah almost peed her pants when Talon warriors started popping into the café like massive black-leather flies. It wasn't so much that she didn't believe what Savage told her—she'd seen Jade throw jets of fire from her hands—she simply didn't have perspective on what it meant. Savage was part of something powerful and important.

Honor. Duty. Sacrifice.

He left his girlfriend to track down and destroy his brother instead of staying put and saying yes to a half-baked proposal to play house. She understood why—truly understood. Lives were at stake in his world, and he sacrificed for what needed to be done.

That didn't make it hurt any less that he'd sacrificed *her*.

Still, she saw the same level of commitment displayed in each of the new faces around the diner. One text that one of their own was threatened and *bam,* they were there.

Like Savage had come for her.

With the Whippoorwill locked down, and massive men appearing in every empty space, it got claustrophobic quickly. Savage led her and Riley straight for one of the biggest men in the room. Older than the rest, he looked no less lethal, despite the fine navy suit and his long, brindle hair.

Reign, he signed. *This is Hannah, the one who saved Cowboy way back when.*

A resounding grunt of approval rose from the warriors surrounding them, and heat crept into her cheeks.

"It's a pleasure, Hannah." Reign took her knuckles to his lips and led the welcome. "I'm sorry we meet under these circumstances."

Hannah swallowed, her neck cranked back to meet Reign's gaze. "I'm sorry. I feel like me calling for Waylon's help dragged everyone into one heck of a mess."

"Nonsense," Waylon said, joining them with Bree wrapped around his hip. "If you hadn't called, you'd be dead, and I would never have forgiven myself."

A dark-haired man with Gothic style and men's eyeliner sauntered over to kiss the brunette that arrived with Savage. "We take care of our own, cowgirl. These rogue wolves didn't understand the whoop-ass they unleashed when they came after you."

"Kobi," Bruin said, lifting his chin. "You're with me. Follow my vapor."

Jade's brother disappeared and the goth guy, Kobi, was gone the next second.

"I'm sorry you're missing your meeting," she said, touching Waylon's arm. "But I'm so relieved you're here."

A flash of hurt clouded Savage's eyes and she felt badly about that. Was it so wrong to take comfort in a friendly face?

Bree growled, staring at where Hannah's hand rested on Waylon's bicep. "Things have changed since the sophomore sock hop, Hannah. Hands off."

Cowboy snorted, kissed Hannah's knuckles, and set her hand on Savage's arm. "Down, coyote girl. I love how you have no idea about the Human Realm. It's adorable. Not to worry, Hannah went to all the dances with Jesse Wilton, a local rodeo hero. It wasn't like that between us, was it, Banana?"

"No," Hannah said, trying not to think about all the summer afternoons she'd watched him in the sun, shirtless, bailing hay. "We're just good friends."

"The best," he said, pulling Bree against his chest and wrapping his arms around her. "Besides, it looks like Hannah roped and tied herself her own bad boy."

Savage flashed him a warning. *Don't say it, Waylon.*

Cowboy made a face. "Oh, I'm sayin' it. You got it bad, Sav. It's written all over your ugly mug. You're in *luuuurve.*"

"Just her flavor of the week," Matt snarked from where he sat on the breakfast bar. "Been there, had that, not much to brag about."

Savage Flashed from Hannah's side, appeared across the room long enough to grab Matt, and then they were gone.

"Ohmigosh," she said, mortified. "Where'd they go? Shouldn't someone follow? Track him? Something?"

"Nah," Jade said, no alarm marring her beautiful, tanned complexion. "Sav will teach him some manners. He's far more civilized than people give him credit for. Cowboy, how about wrapping this dog and pony show up so we can get home? My boobs are killing me. I gotsta feed my babies soon, or I'm gonna bust."

Waylon laughed and straightened to address the room. "'Kay, so, out of deep respect for Jade's aching breasts, let's get this over with."

Jade nodded. Reign rolled his eyes, but Hannah could tell he adored them all.

"Bree, Savage, and I will stay here and sort out this pack bullshit. Everybody else heads home."

"Done deal," Reign said.

Cowboy knuckle bumped with the massive warrior and turned to Jade. "Hey, Blaze, can I impose upon you to offer Hannah a place to stay while we sort out her farm and insurance and shit? My mate will get territorial if I invite another woman into the Dens. And she bites."

Bree punched him in the stomach, and he laughed like he expected it. The laughter in him soothed a worry Hannah had carried inside her for over a decade. He really was happy.

Jade grabbed her coat from a booth and straightened, shoving her arms in the sleeves. "Of course. If Hannah's home, Savage is too. Win-

win. Happy to have you and Riley both. I'll let Elora know we'll have three more for dinner."

"Can we make that five?" the brunette asked. "If Savage is home and Kobi's in Africa, Aust and I would love to join you."

Reign nodded. "Elora will love that."

Savage Flashed back into the diner and his smug smile raised the hair on her arms. "Where's Matt?"

In a remote village in Syria, nursing a broken nose. He shrugged. *What? It'll do him good to understand what it feels like to be caught up in a war he has nothing to do with.*

"A life lesson in the real world." Jade laughed, zipped up her coat, and freed her long, red locks. "So, we'll see you all at dinner. I look forward to having you, Hannah."

Hannah's head spun by the time the majority of Savage's friends poofed out of the room. Left behind were the angry and frightened faces of friends and neighbors she'd known her entire life.

"What now, Way—Cowboy? What happens to them?"

Cowboy shrugged. "What do you think should happen, HB? You're the one most affected here."

She felt bad for them. Whatever happened, it had been the actions of a few, not all. She met Jayne's worried gaze, where she sat with Sue and Mark Immery, and wished none of this had happened. "They aren't all bad. Most of them just happen to turn into wolves. Please don't punish the many for the actions of the few."

You realize they kidnapped your sister, tried to kill you three times, and blew up your house, right?

Savage's protective fury didn't surprise her. "The majority of these people know us. I have to believe they didn't want to hurt Riley or me. Some are hotheads at the best of times, granted, but most are friends . . . at least on my side of things. I just want that to be a consideration."

Cowboy exhaled and looked around at the worried faces. "Okay, let's get a roster of who's left and maybe you can help me go over it. I have no interest in being their Alpha, but I'll be damned if I leave them lost and abandoned. Weres are only as strong as their pack."

Hannah nodded, relieved and thankful Cowboy was still the boy she knew so long ago. "And I'm so glad you found your pack."

~

It was one of those days that never wanted to end. With my powers unlocked, Hannah's grief clutched my heart with the same crippling strength as if it were my own. Sifting through the remnants of her family home felt like I was tied down with fire ants gnawing at my groin. Painful. Uncomfortable. And as much as I wanted to yell and flail and fight, there was nothing to be done but endure.

With heat hemorrhaging from the burnt foundation and the scent of charred wood filling my nostrils, I searched the destruction, fruitlessly trying to salvage some remnant of her life that would soothe her.

Riley tromped over with a pathetic handful of charred belongings hanging at her side and a scowl on her young face. "This is bullshit. Those wolves should be neutered and strung up and then neutered again."

"Language, Ri," Hannah mumbled.

"Language my Aunt Fanny. Neutered isn't a curse word. Besides, between the fire and the water and the snow, our life is wrecked. What's the sense of standing around? It's just making you sad. Mom always said, if you're going through a rough patch, don't dwell. Get moving, and get clear."

Hannah nodded, her tears creating clean tracks in the soot that covered her face. "That was her motto, all right. I thought about that when she first left my dad and me. I guess that approach worked for her."

I winced, as Riley took the brunt of the hit. Poor kid. Cowboy was on it. He waved her over to him and Bree. "Ri-ri, come see what we found under this heap of timber. Look."

The three of them proceeded to excavate a fire-safe from under the rubble. Hopefully, it was full to bursting with pictures and mementos and other irreplaceables. They exhumed the treasure from the rubble and set it beside an heirloom chair. Hannah's gran had hand-stitched the needlepoint seat, and it had been their only miraculous save.

When Hannah's tears gained ground, she sought shelter in my arms. "Riley's right. I'm numb, and I can't breathe. I keep searching for Chief, hoping and hoping not to find him. Can we just go?"

I nodded and kissed her cheek. With a whistle to get everyone's attention, I signaled our retreat for the night.

An hour later, I sat on the bed of the guest room Jade had set up for Hannah. Fresh from the shower and thankful to have my own clothes on, I waited for her to finish up with the spray revival and face the world. She'd been in there a long time. Like, eons long. Like, something's very wrong long. But that was the point. Something *was* very wrong, so I left her to her mourning.

"Hey," Riley said, sticking her head in from the hall. "I'm going for the tour with Cowboy. Can you tell Hannah I'll meet her downstairs at dinner?"

I raised my hands to check on how she was doing, but she wouldn't understand. It felt hollow to give her a thumbs up after losing her home and her dog and being kidnapped, but it was what it was.

Maybe she sensed my disappointment, or saw my desire to connect. Either way, when she came in and wrapped her arms around my neck, I latched on for the hug.

"Thank you for saving us. And for bringing us here. And for loving Hannah. She's been sad for a long time. She hasn't said anything, but I can tell you hurt her the first time around. Don't do that again, okay?"

I squeezed her tight and then pulled back drawing an X over my chest. *Cross my heart.*

As Riley headed out, I thought about Jade's offer to help work on my vocal cords. Could I speak again? I was pretty sure all I'd have to do is ask Castian, and it would be done. Taking the easy way out had never been my thing. Besides, if Riley learned to sign, she could talk to both me and Coal. Then, everyone I cared about was accessible. Maybe I didn't need to change everything all at once.

I laid back on the bed and closed my eyes. It had been a long time since I considered the future. It had never been about what I wanted from it but what I thought I deserved.

I never imagined I deserved much.

When my twin stole my powers and doubled his strength, I felt like the destruction Abaddon and the Scourge caused was my fault. I felt like a failure. Unworthy of love and a happy ending because people suffered.

Hannah spun me around.

Hannah was my muse. My mate. My love. My life.

Drifting off in a half-daze, I recognized the power she held over me. I worked with magical people every day, and not one of them held me in thrall or altered my course or turned my life into knots like Hannah.

She was beautiful . . . strong . . . feisty . . .

Warm lips on the scar crossing my throat woke me from a dream I didn't want to slip away. My heart stilled for half a beat until the fog cleared. Hannah, naked and straddled over my hips, undid my belt, her gaze soft and sad.

"I need you."

I broke from the kiss to check the door. Closed.

"Everything hurts." She tugged my shirt free from my jeans and shoved it up and over my head.

Puffy red eyes, her hair towel dried and unbrushed, her shoulders curled with exhaustion. I was speechless. My poor, beautiful Hannah.

"I can't breathe. Please, make it stop for a while."

Anything. Everything. If Hannah wanted for anything, I wanted to be her go-to guy. Rolling her to the side, I grabbed the condoms from my pocket, pulled my pants past my hips, and saw-kicked them until they flopped on the floor.

The heated, hungry sex we had over the past three days was great, but *this* is what I wanted.

Time to reacquaint ourselves.

Touching more than her curves.

Trusting me to fend off the world when things hit home.

Rolling her onto her back, I followed the momentum and caged her beneath the shelter of my body. Pressed into the mattress, with her arms around my neck, and her legs parted enough to cradle my hips, she stole the last of my self-preservation.

I bit my lip instead of mouthing the words burning my tongue. She didn't want declarations of love from me.

Show, don't tell, right?"

Making love to Hannah—truly out-of-body tending to her soul— was the single-most enlightening honor I ever experienced. Trapped in the dark, fighting shadows, Hannah showed me the glimmer of something different three years ago. Secrets kept me at a distance then. Now, she knew everything about me, my life, and my world. All I had to do was convince her to open up to me again.

Hannah's hips rose up, urging me to get out of my head and inside her. Ripping the foil square with my teeth, I freed the condom and held it up for her to claim. She had a thing for rolling them on, and I wouldn't deprive her of even that pleasure.

Slowly, the tip of my erection slid into place and I sheathed myself in her body. I let out a ragged breath.

Heaven. This was my heaven.

CHAPTER ELEVEN

*B*y dawn the next morning, we were mucking stalls, slugging feed, and getting things done. Being in the barn, breathing Hannah's bizarre scents of comfort, and drowning her thoughts with the constant droning bellows of cattle, seemed more therapeutic than anything I'd done for her up to that point . . . well, maybe not *anything*.

I earned my nom de guerre last night.

After taking her, fresh from the shower, we'd spent an hour at dinner making nice with my family, and then retired for an endless session of healing, tears, and the kind of sex that branded two people. Somewhere on the tender flesh of her heart, I was certain I left my mark.

She asked me for sex. I gave her much more.

Men generally ran out of steam. With Hannah, I never did. She sought me out in her half-sleep, finding my naked body in the sheets over and over again through the night. Each time, I soothed her aches and sated her needs without question, complaint, or hesitation.

I was engaged—truly vested in winning her back. Whatever walls and safety nets had separated us the first time around were blown to rubble gone. I cast a side-eyed glance to check on her from where I was patching a wood rail that got snapped in yesterday's fight.

She caught me looking at her and smiled. "You swing a nine-pound hammer like nobody's business, you know that?"

Yeah, I did. My dedication to mend what had been damaged went far beyond a broken pen rail. I finished with another few nails and realized she was still checking me out. Setting my tools down, I raised my hands. *Do you need something, doc?*

In my mind, she smiled and said something sexy like "Just you," but in reality, she shook her head. It was coming, though. I could feel it. Her growing need to lean on me wasn't only because life had worn her thin.

Yes, she needed the support, but when I opened my arms, she came forward as if drawn in like steel to a super-magnet. I would hold her for as long as it took.

My phone vibrated in my pocket. I checked the message, and then handed it to her so she could read the screen. "What does Waylon mean, HB is all good?"

Cowboy caught the ranch up at the bank and paid for next month. My finger on her lip contained the burst of her protest. *I told him you wouldn't be cool with that. He said, if you insist, you can pay him back once the insurance is settled and you and Riley have decided how you want to proceed.*

"I insist. We're not a charity."

No one thinks that.

"I don't want his money."

I sighed, but it was nothing I hadn't expected. *I would have done it myself but Cowboy seized the pack accounts under his father's name and used those. He's not out of pocket, and you can't deny those wolves owe you for pain and suffering.*

Even so, I knew she wouldn't take what wasn't hers. "When the insurance is settled, I'm paying him back. The pack families will need it to rebuild."

I shrugged. That was between her and Cowboy now. I'd play it her way, no matter what came next.

"Okay, let's go outside, and see what they've managed to salvage. I'm tired of the cold and want to explore your mountain more. Was Aust serious when he said he needed to introduce us to the wolves of Haven?"

I flipped the metal gate latch, securing the pen, and patted the cow that bleated. Finished with the cattle, we headed out to the horse stalls. *Aust's wolves are part of our first level security. They aren't like Werewolves. They are forest wolves that Aust and Zo communicate with. I promise you'll be safe, and Riley will get a kick out of it.*

Riley would get a kick out of anything Aust said or did, with or without wolves. The Highborne seemed to have stolen her heart over one family dinner. Then again, Aust had one of the gentlest souls I'd ever come across.

"Okay, let's get this over with, and we'll go meet the wolves."

Waylon, Bree, and Zophia, had escorted us to the farm earlier and, while the two of us took care of chores, the support team dealt with the snow-dusted smolders of her life.

With my gloved fingers linked with hers, Hannah seemed to steel herself for the breath-sucking gut punch of looking at the rubble of her family home.

I felt her grief hit as sharply as it had yesterday.

"Hannah, come see what we did, sweetheart." Cowboy waved her over to where he and Zophia were salvaging.

She strode forward, determination in every stride. "I *heard* what you did and I'm paying you back. Don't even think of fighting me on it."

Cowboy hugged her as they met up and waved her rant away. Excitement sparked in his eyes and wind lifted his flaxen hair. "Yeah, yeah. Whatevs. Just know there's no rush. My pack and my parents owe you that much."

She stepped back and sighed. "You look so much like your mother and brother, it amazes me. Except, you have a genuine playfulness that nobody in your pack or family have."

I felt how that weighed her heart down.

"Don't be sad on my account, sweetheart. Everything worked out exactly as it was meant to, thanks to you." He waited until that sank in, then shook her arm and pointed toward the truck. "Wait until you see what Zo did."

She followed his line of sight to the furniture and boxes stacked in the back of her old, beater truck. The slipper chair from beside her bed. A pine dough box. Her washstand. All her most cherished pieces in pristine condition. "What? I don't understand. What's in the boxes?"

"Your belongings," Zophia said, raising her hands to catch the whips of chestnut hair striking her face. She frowned. As if she commanded the wind itself, the air grew still around them. "As the Keeper of Lives in Progress, I deemed your losses unacceptable. I therefore return the things which mean the most to you."

Hannah swallowed, her eyes wide. "Is this possible?"

The soul-crushing loss of her family history eased and I sent a private thanks to Zo. The loss of the house was terrible, and cleaved her in two, but the memories tied to her heirlooms meant so much more to her.

I wiped her tears and kissed her cheek. *We'll store your things and rebuild. Just like it was. I can fix this for you, doc. There were too many witnesses to the fire to magically undo the destruction, but once time passes, Zo and I will ask Castian to put your home back. I'll work the farm while you finish your vet schooling, I'll help Riley with her homework so you can get back to who and what you want to be. You asked me to stay once, and I didn't . . . please, ask me again.*

The tears that warmed my palms gained momentum. Were they happy tears? There, in front of my BFF and sister, I pledged my future to her. My support. My love. I sorted out my stuff and came back stronger than ever.

"No," she said, her voice tripping over emotion. Wrapping herself around my chest, she sobbed against my leather jacket. "No, that's not what I want."

Her words hung in the still, cold air and my mind went numb. No. Always no. My heart shattered behing my ribs. Maybe I never had a shot of winning her back. Maybe her heart was lost to me from the moment I walked away.

"Uh . . . we'll give you two a sec, 'kay?" The sadness on Cowboy's face as he and Zo turned toward the truck sealed the deal. This was a dead-end and I was the last to realize it.

Hannah grew stiff in my arms and pulled back. When she saw the tears brimming my eyes, she gasped and gripped my jaw in both her hands. "No no no, I'm sorry, that came out wrong. I want *you*, yes. I want you to stay with me, but no, I don't want to be tied to this farm and the cattle and a vet practice."

What? I searched her face hard to make sure I didn't just hear what I wanted. *You want me? You trust me to fix what I broke?*

"Stay with me, Savage. Be my family."

I pinched my eyes tight, and the built-up tears fell.

Hannah popped up on her toes to give me a quick kiss. "For the first time in my life, my family obligations have lifted. I don't want it to be the same as it was, I want to join you in your world. I want to travel and laugh with your family, and leave this lonely landscape, for love."

I swiped rough fingers over my eyes, and she read my next question without a word passing between us.

"I'm sure. Like you said about being a soldier, being a country girl is *who* I am, not where. I miss having people in my life, and squabbles and opinions and all the glorious chaos that comes with family. I want that for Riley. I want babies and cousins, and didn't even realize how much until dinner last night. Your family is an inspiring mishmash of personalities and, from what I gathered, there are many more additions I haven't even gotten to know yet."

Can we ask Riley to give up her world and her friends?

Hannah laughed. "Last night, she pestered Reign about enrolling in his academy all through dessert. Then, she went out and rode a giant black panther through the woods with three handsome elves, a Werewolf, and his coyote wife. I'm sure she'll be fine."

A piercing whistle had us turning to where Cowboy stood at the truck. "Bree's back, and she found something you lost yesterday."

"Chief!" Hannah bolted toward the ball of black-and-white fur, curled in Bree's arms. Her pup let off a whine as she set him on the tailgate of the truck. "He's hurt. How bad?"

Bree shrugged. "I'm not sure. I tracked him a couple of miles west and found him in a culvert under a side road, curled up to die. He's weak, but Jade can fix him up if his injuries aren't natural."

"I've got this, HB." Cowboy scooped her dog up and disappeared in the next instant. Bree followed her mate.

"What does that mean?" Hannah asked, searching my face, her expression pleading.

I gathered her shaking hands and gave them a gentle squeeze. *Magic isn't all-encompassing. There is a balance to all things and a price to be paid for altering a course. Jade's magical healing costs her a great deal of energy, but if a patient's condition is due to natural causes, nothing she does will change the outcome.*

"So, I'm actually hoping my dog got hurt by the wolves? That seems a little sadistic, doesn't it?"

Savage chuckled. *Our world isn't perfect, doc. Most days, we hope for the best and prepare for a kick to the groin. If Jade's able, Chief will live. If not, Bree's lion brothers, Rhys and Bram, will do their best. They're our resident animal medics.*

Hannah rubbed the center of her chest.

"Too much?" Zo asked, her gaze a solid comfort.

Hannah looked anguished. "The coyote's brothers are lions? The people of Haven seemed to open their homes and their families and take in any strays which needed a home."

I nodded. *That's pretty much it.*

Her smile suggested she liked that idea. "I'm ready to go back, but all my stuff . . . and I need to go to the police station, and then . . . I'm selling the cattle."

Zo squeezed her hand. "I'll collect Riley and we can watch over Chief and keep you posted. There's nothing you can do there, so finish here and come home when you can."

Hannah hugged Zo and lingered in the embrace.

I hoped they would be even closer than girlfriends. Maybe, one day soon, they'd be sisters.

EPILOGUE

*T*wo weeks later

I reined my horse to a stop, dismounted, and tied the beast off on the rail post. Pointing up the sun-washed slope of the mountain, I indicated our final destination. Several hundred feet above, the shadowed entrance of the Dens sat almost hidden in the rocky tip of the mountain rise.

The plateau for the Dens is quite a hike. Are you sure you don't want me to Flash us up there?

Hannah tied off Whisky Jack and grabbed the gift bag. She spent all morning fussing and fluffing the tissue, getting it just right. I didn't see the point when they would just rip it open, but whatevs.

"Flashing makes you lazy. With the amount of booze you and your boys drink, you'll all be sporting paunches if you don't work it off. Fight the beer belly, husband." She smacked my rock-hard abs, and she and Chief jogged up the first steps of the steep stone path.

I laughed and ran to catch up. *Husband.*

I would never tire of hearing her call me that. The ceremony was small—two dozen people, a ton of food, and a new tattoo for each of us. She chose the Talon hawk with Savage clutched in the raptor's claws, and I chose a spiked mace with Hannah written in flourish beneath. She got the ball-and-chain reference immediately, and that was one of the many reasons I was ass over end in love with her.

She got me.

Smiling like an idiot, I took pleasure in the view of her ass in those painted on jeans. Working the slope, those muscled legs, the firm globes of her ass . . . yep, and just like that, I was rock hard and ready.

Gods, how had I survived without her? I swear, I never drew breath into my lungs until she said she loved me. Now, I was in-fuck-ing-vincible.

Let the world come at me—I was ready and steady.

Let the three realms explode around us—we stood on solid ground. Sure, my god powers sizzled in the slurry of my cells, but that wasn't the fuel to my fire. Hannah was my be-all-end-all. And Riley topped my life sundae, making every single thing in the world more perfect.

"So, who all lives up here?" she asked, pausing to catch her breath.

Bruin and Mika, the four orphaned lion cubs they took in, Mika's grand-father. Cowboy and Bree. A Puma who works as their nanny. The guards. Pretty much any Were who wants or needs a home.

When we reached the top, Bruin stood grinning at the top of the steps. In a tight t-shirt despite the damp January chill, his thick arms and chest threatened to bust loose of their cotton restraints. The bear seemed to have swollen in size since yesterday, and given the reason for our visit, I didn't doubt he had.

Bear. Congrats, my man.

Bruin met me chest-to-chest and thumped my back. "Thanks. Mika did the hard part and rocked it like you read about. Seriously, that female amazes me more every fucking day."

I know what you mean.

"Yeah, you do." Bruin winked and bent to kiss Hannah's cheek. "Welcome to my home, Hannah. Come in and see what we made."

Chief trotted off along the plateau path that wrapped the mountain, so Bruin told the guards standing sentinel to watch over him. I pointed up, and paused long enough in the rotunda foyer to allow Hannah to read the missive Mika hand-painted along the ceiling line.

We believe in the right to bear arms and the right to arm BEARS.

"Hannah!" Cowboy ran to greet her, scooped her up, and swung her around. "Welcome to our home."

Bruin laughed. "I already covered that, Waylon."

Cowboy moaned, and I got my hands moving. *Get used to it. You're not living that name down for the next decade. It's a bit over the top country twang, don't you think?*

"Like I had any say in the matter."

"Play nice, boys." Hannah's smile when she slid her arm around my back and linked her thumb into my beltloop nearly did me in. Gods, at this rate, I would need to cut this short and find a private spot to keep the honeymoon rolling.

"Bruin, tell me. How long was Mika's labor?"

Bruin gestured past the huge harvest table in the dining room and down the hall. "All in, twenty-one hours, but only seven or eight of that was actually hard labor."

"Says the male who sat, watched, and cracked jokes." Mika rolled her eyes as we entered the great room. Seated on one of the leather couches sipping tea, she pointed over to the playpen set up near the fireplace.

"Don't water down my whiskey, woman," Bruin said, feigning insult. "I was a great birthing coach. Cowboy, back me up here."

Hannah ignored the banter, bypassed the playpen, and went straight for the new mother. "You look wonderful, Mika. Congratulations."

And she did. Aside from seeming a little tired, with her hair pulled back and wearing a t-shirt that Bruin had undoubtedly bought reading, "Grin and bear it," Mika was as radiant as ever.

I left the women to unwrap the gift and talk about pushing and whatnot, and headed over to see the new arrivals. Amongst the ivory blankets, with their little eyes closed, and skin bare except for the fuzz of fur to come, lay three baby bears that would each fit into the palm of my hand.

Triplets? Bruin and his twin, Gemma, had been born after Risa and her twin, Emma. I was expecting two.

"Surprise!" Bruin laughed. "Yep. We thought we had it wrapped up after Briar and Bowen were locked down and then, *bam*, Braydon shot out."

"Shot out?" Mika scowled at him. "Were you even in the same room as me? You're unbelievable."

Bruin snorted and waved away her censure. "So, yeah, triplet boys to add to the chaos of the quads we inherited."

As if on cue, three lion cubs came barreling through the room mrowling and hissing, swatting each other with Kiara toddling after them at a run. "No bother da babies," she shouted, waggling her finger. "Babies seeping."

Bruin jogged over and scooped the little girl into his arms. "You tell them, princess. Boys, playroom if you're roughhousing. Go on."

Kiara placed her palms against Bruin's cheeks and beamed. "I take good care of da babies."

He kissed her forehead and snuggled her into his neck. The sweet girl purred loudly, her tight, golden locks resting against his tanned skin. "Yes, you do, my little lovie. You're a great big sister."

"And you have lots of brothers to watch over," Hannah said, joining them. She brushed the back of her finger gently over one of the boys and smiled. "Oh, goodness. They are so adorable."

"They're adorable when they're lying there growing," Mika said, raising her hands to the stone ceiling, "but may the Earth Mother give me strength—six boys?"

Bruin laughed again and tossed Kiara into the air making her squeal. "Don't tally things up yet, baby. This is only our first litter. We've got plenty of time to—" The thud of Mika's shoe to Bruin's gut made them all laugh. "What? Too soon?"

Hannah passed Riley a second helping of honeyed pastries and tried, yet again, to take it all in. Elora's cooking, Jade's hospitality, Were babies, warrior friends, the Highbornes, magic, the Realm of the Fair —the list was endless. And awesome. She meant that in the truest sense of the word. She looked around, filled with such an over-whelming sense of awe she didn't know what to do with it.

It filled her up and yet terrified her at the same time. How did she fit? What was her purpose here? Everything was different, yet funda-mentally the same.

It was *soooo* much.

Preoccupied with her mind swirl, she missed something said at the table and Riley tapped her arm. "Hmm, I'm sorry?" she said, searching the expectant faces around the table.

Zophia's warrior mate, the Goth demon, smiled and put her out of her misery. "Zo and Sav have a surprise for you. If you're finished with dinner, we're taking a walk."

She glanced at Riley. Her sister's shrug suggested that she too was in the dark. Rising from her seat, Chief got up and shook himself out, ready for the outing.

February rains had dissolved all but the most determined patches of snow, and though the ground was mucky, it remained frozen beneath the surface. They took the path that led toward Zophia's massive home in the ancient rune clearing, and everyone chatted amongst themselves.

Aust had Riley walked with a massive russet wolf named Nightrunner. Zophia, Bree, and Jade chatted about Jade's twins. Kobi, Galan, and Cowboy whispered about something. And she, again, tried to take it all in. She said she wanted the chaos of family.

Be careful what you wish for, right?

Savage squeezed her hand, checking in with her as he often did. *Are you good?* he asked with his look.

She nodded. Too good was probably the best answer.

There was a loud *whoooop* in the air a moment before Aust reached his arms out and caught an incoming ape. The animal swung in from a low-hanging branch and met his chest with a trust that spoke of how often he must've caught her in the past. "Hello, *sweeting*, did you miss me? Riley, this is Hoola."

Riley raised her hand, and the little ape squeezed her finger. The smile on her face made Hannah's year. Man, this life offered her sister so many more experiences. She needed to remember that. Sometimes she worried that uprooting them and moving was selfish on her part.

Then, in moments like these, that worry eased.

"I took a similar walk to this a few years ago," Jade said, falling into step with her. "I hope it works out as well for you as it did for me."

Hannah was about to ask what she meant when the group stopped and parted. In front of her sat a sprawling bungalow cabin, with large windows glowing warm from within and a trail of smoke rising from the fireplace. "What's this?" she asked. "Who lives here?"

We do, Savage signed. *Come inside and see.*

Holding her hand, he led her to the front step where he whisked her into his arms and over the threshold. In the foyer, he set her back on her feet and started signing. *Four bedrooms, two fireplaces, a big open concept country kitchen and living room combo. It's not as big as Jade's or Zo's homes, by any means, but I thought—"*

"I don't care about big," she said, toeing off her boots so she didn't track mud. Tears warmed her cheeks as she rushed forward and stroked the surface of her beloved antique table.

He'd never be a wine-and-roses kind of man, but Savage showed her he loved her in different ways—the squeeze of her hand, her gran's vase bursting with hydrangeas, the warmth of colors, the attention to detail.

Like a kid on Christmas morning, she searched the rooms, each time finding more of her things unpacked and placed with such thought and attention, her chest ached. Savage's love language was something you had to learn to understand but once you did, you realized he spoke as loudly as any other man ever could.

"Thank you. But do you want to move out? You've told me a dozen times how glad you are to be home."

It's nice to see everyone on the regular, but that won't change if we have our own place. My heart is at home with you. Your heart is at home with your things and your family. Here, we can both have what fills our souls.

She blinked at him and nodded. He understood her on a level she never expected. "How about we invite everyone in out of the rain and start this housewarming?"

His smile lit her up inside. *The sooner they come in, the sooner they leave. Then we start christening the rooms. Did I tell you I can now cast privacy spells? All the sounds of lovemaking and no teen embarrassment in the morning.*

She burst out laughing and threw her arms around his neck. "You've thought of everything, tough guy. It's perfect."

The End

AFTERWORD

Thank You For Reading
I sincerely hope you enjoyed Savage and Hannah's story in, *Savage Love*. If you'd like to share your thoughts on the novel please leave a rating or review on Amazon. Reviews help other readers find books. I appreciate all reviews and look forward to reading your thoughts.
In gratitude,
JL

ABOUT THE AUTHOR

Author Notes
Written on 03/10/2019

Thank you so much for reading, and since you're reading this—for continuing to read. I know how valuable time is in this life and am honored you entrusted your precious hours with my characters.

When I finished Scourge Survivor Series at book 5, I thought I'd wrapped things up. Five strong women, five elements of nature to master, five love stories. But as I wrote Fate's Journey, it became apparent that there were too many characters who mattered to wrap up everyone's lives.

Savage was one character who many readers asked about. Being the toughest, broodiest warrior, he needed to find his happily ever after too. I hope you enjoyed it.

If you have any thoughts or comments, feel free to email me. I'm always eager to chat. If you like my writing and want to try out one of the other series, I welcome your feedback on those too.

If you're wondering about my Dark Angels Paranormal Series, I've enclosed a few pages of Book 1, Watcher Untethered, for you to read. Enjoy,

JL

ALSO BY JL MADORE

Find Me:

Social Media – Facebook, Twitter, Instagram

Web page – www.jlmadore.com

Email – jlmadorewrites@gmail.com

Reader Group – JL Series Updates

JL's Reverse Harem Titles

Guardians of the Fae Realms

Guardians of the Phoenix – Calli's Harem

Book 1 – Rise of the Phoenix

Book 2 – Wolf's Soul

Book 3 – Bear's Strength

Book 4 – Hawk's Heart

Book 5 – Jaguar's Passion

Darkness Calls – Keyla's harem

Book 6 – Dark Curse

Book 7 – Dark Soul

Book 8 – Dark Crown

Guardians of the Crown – Honor's Harem

Book 9 – Honor Restored

Book 10 – Honor Guards

Book 11 – Honor Bound

Book 12 – Honor Empowered

Rise of the Amberloq – Lark's Harem

Book 13 – Find the Fallen

Book 14 – Rise from Ruin

Book 15 – Trust and Triumph

Exemplar Hall – Jesse's Harem

Book 1 – Captured by the Magi

Book 2 – Jesse and the Magi Vault

Book 3 – The Makings of a Magi Knight

Book 4 – Clash with the Magi Council

Book 5 – The Unstoppable Storme

JL's More Traditional M/F, M/M, or Menage

The Watchers of the Gray Series (Paranormal)

Watchers of the Gray Boxset – Complete Series

Book 1 – Watcher Untethered – Zander

Book 2 – Watcher Redeemed – Kyrian

Book 3 – Watcher Reborn – Danel

Book 4 – Watcher Divided – Phoenix

Book 5 – Watcher United – Seth

Book 6 – Watcher Compelled – Bo

Book 7 – Watcher Unfeigned – Brennus

Book 8 – Watcher Exposed – Taharqa

The Scourge Survivor Series (Fantasy)

Scourge Survivor Series Boxset - Complete Series

Book 1 – Blaze Ignites

Book 2 – Ursa Unearthed

Book 3 – Torrent of Tears

Book 4 – Blind Spirit

Book 5 – Fate's Journey

Book 6 – Savage Love – epilogue novella

Aliens of Atlantis Series (Sci-Fi)

Book 1 – Taryn's Tiderider

Book 2 – Kai's Captive

Book 3 – Alyandra's Shadow

DARK ANGELS PARANORMAL SERIES - WATCHER UNTETHERED

"This asshole's head is mine. I mean it, Tanek."

Zander swerved the truck down a shadowed side street, the squeal of rubber on road echoing off brick buildings. The dark fury in his blood had him lit to explode. That he could even drive astonished him. He couldn't believe any Otherworlder—Dark or Light—could be so massively stupid.

"He's headed for that alley, Z. Get closer." Tanek popped the passenger door open and swung out onto the step bar. "Man, this one's quick."

Quick? The pro-wrestler build of their bad guy was deceiving as hell, because boots to asphalt, the daemon ran Usain Bolt fast—even with the added weight of an unconscious blonde slung over his shoulder.

A growl rumbled deep in Zander's chest. Nothing ranked lower in his playbook of evil than daemons who preyed on innocent females, except maybe a daemon who preyed on innocent females who happened to be at his nightclub.

Zander strangled the steering wheel as his foot ground harder on the gas. As the Navigator's engine revved, he banked a hard left down the alley. The tires screamed into the night and he almost lost Tanek.

The space between the buildings was tight, the walls zipping past on both sides of the truck in a blur.

There wasn't much in life or death Zander cared about—except maybe pissing people off. Celestial guardian. Soulless assassin. Despised bastard. Meh, all one and the same. He was Nephilim, and this daemon would be schooled in what it meant to provoke a Soldier of the Choir.

"My club is a safe zone, Tanek. My house. My kill."

"*Victori spolia*," Tanek said, launching off the side of the truck. His size fourteens landed heavy, his momentum pitching him into a run.

"To the victor goes the spoils, my ass." Zander stomped the brakes and slammed the shifter into park. He bailed out and tore down the alley after his commander. The guy's leather vest flared like a cape behind him, the Nephilim runes etched into the back, glimmering silver under the lights of the sleeping city.

Lost in the shadows, Tanek unsheathed his blade and Zander followed his lead. Three a.m. in an industrial section of Toronto's fashion district left few humans to witness the excitement, but it only took one industrious looky-loo with a cell phone and the Otherworld was exposed and going viral on the internet.

"She isn't human," Tanek said, over his shoulder. "Could be worse."

Zander checked the sightlines from the rooftops and wondered how Tanek did it. The guy still spouted optimism and he'd been trapped in this thankless existence longer than any of them. They barreled through another back alley and spooked a pair of scavenging raccoons. The rotund little bandits scattered in a flurry of hostile chatter.

Yeah, human would be worse.

One tenet galvanized all members of the Otherworld. It had nothing to do with character alignment or their feeding needs, whether blood, flesh, spirit, or fear. It had everything to do with the food *source*.

Humans must remain oblivious.

The two of them hurdled overgrown boxwoods, their boots propelling them through backstreets, around graffiti-covered dumpsters and over broken wooden skids littering their path. Most nights, obstacles kept the chase interesting, but tonight, Zander wanted to skip the calisthenics and get straight to the decapitating part.

Shit. They'd lost visual.

Tanek vaulted over a concrete barricade and signaled for Zander to flank left and cover the next building. Zander changed course. They weren't out of this. The only place the daemon could take cover was in the cluster of dilapidated, two-storey warehouses ahead. Working a quick and dirty grid, they melted into the overcast night, cranked door handles, and eyeballed what windows they found.

Zander focused his energy and summoned his gift. With a low-level current arcing within his cells, he scanned the area, his senses heightened. He itched to detect the acrid scent of daemon. He strained for any movement shift or the faintest rustle in the distance. He sensed—nothing.

August air hung deathly still and heavy in his lungs; no breeze to carry scents and no sound of movement to point them in the right direction. He wiped a wrist across his brow and cursed. The storm brewing over Lake Ontario flashed angry strobes and threatened its wrath.

As he ghosted across the next loading ramp, his electrical mojo did its thing and his head cranked around. Zeroing in on a piece-of-shit factory two units over, the hair on the nape of his neck stood at attention. *Gotcha.*

Zander whistled for Tanek to follow and pistoned forward.

The building stood an inspired tribute to post-war ramshackle and as he back-flatted against the red brick, clay detritus crumbled onto the walkway. He sidestepped toward the metal door and sucked in a lungful—

Fuck. The stench of death and ode-to-campfire tunneled into his sinuses—the all too familiar mix of rotting human flesh, terror, and brimstone. A daemon kill-zone.

Now, the trip into industrial-landia made sense. Isolated after dark. No nosy neighbors to hear baleful screams from within. And no way for him and Tanek to guess how many of Hell Realm's army lurked inside.

While his lungs sucked in more incentive to decapitate, Zander retrieved the Moonstone from his vest pocket. In the heartbeat it took Tanek to join the party, Zander brushed a thumb across the feldspar and uttered the words to fire the ancient runes to life. Heaven's light erupted from the stone and sliced the darkness.

Good to go. Well, aside from having no idea what species of daemon they faced *aaaand* the fact that this whole snatch-and-chase scenario made his skin tingle. On that thought, he retrieved his phone and messaged Kyrian their location.

Ironically, the bigger the army inside, the better it was for the kidnapped female—cocky daemons were stupid daemons. No matter what flesh-eater species they chased, if that asshole had his entire nest inside, he'd be less likely to open a portal back to Hell and take his victim to go. And no way was he making off with his catch of the night.

Tanek grabbed the steel door handle and raised a three-finger count.

Three. Two. One.

www.ingramcontent.com/pod-product-compliance
Lightning Source LLC
Chambersburg PA
CBHW052145170626
46812CB00004B/1596